The Doctor and the Clown

Also by Mario Milosevic

Novels
Claypot Dreamstance
The Coma Monologues
Kyle's War
The Last Giant
Splitting
Terrastina and Mazolli

Collections
15 Strange Tales of Crime and Mystery
Entangled Realities (with Kim Antieau)
Labor Days
Miniatures

Poetry
Animal Life
Fantasy Life
Love Life

The Doctor
and
the Clown

Mario Milosevic

Green Snake
PUBLISHING

It is a curious fact that people are never so trivial as when they take themselves seriously.

Oscar Wilde

"Did you ever want to kill one of your patients?"

As idle bus chatter, I had to admit, that line was more than a little arresting. The man who asked me the question was perfectly sincere in his curiosity, sitting in the window seat, practically daring me, with his question, to take the aisle seat next to him. At first I didn't know how to answer. With a truth? With the lie? Or some combination of the two? Or even if I *should* answer.

I was on my way home to Portland from Seattle where I was supposed to have been attending a conference on communicable diseases but where I actually spent most of my time with high-priced prostitutes. Nothing I'm proud of, but there it is. My life needed that kind of excitement and I will not apologize for it, though I will hold a tiny measure of shame in my heart for my actions. You can imagine me sheltering it like a polished stone. Perhaps that will give you some consolation, as it does me.

On my last night in Seattle, after my consort and I were finished with our activities and she was getting ready to leave, I asked her if it would be all right for me to request her services again, the next time I was in town. I could see my question gave her pause. She wanted to say yes—after all, her profession is predicated on a willingness to please—but she forced herself to say the truth.

"I don't think so."

"Did I do something to offend you?" I asked.

"No, it's not that. You have this—need—I'm not sure how to describe it."

I never wanted to force myself on anyone, least of all the very accommodating women who saw to my desires with discretion and gratifying energy, so I was perfectly willing to let her go, despite the fact that I found her most charming indeed. I even wanted to know her real name, which in the world of such transactions is completely lacking in social graces, as you can imagine. But there was something about the way she declined my request. As though I scared her.

"May I ask what need I could possibly have that would frighten you so completely?"

"It's nothing. There are other girls you can request."

"I know that," I said, a certain impatience creeping into my words, which I regretted. "But I am intrigued by your reaction." I spread my hands. "I really want to know."

She looked at me with a calculating gaze. I could see she wanted to leave. I was not holding her, by any means, but I hoped she wouldn't go, at least not for the next few minutes.

Then, reluctantly: "You want something we can't really give you. Or don't want to give you."

"And what's that?"

"You want things to die, I think."

I laughed. "Preposterous. I'm a doctor."

She raised her eyebrows. "Really? A doctor? I'm surprised."

"Why?"

"Because I could sense it in you, this desire. You aren't interested in living. You want everything around you to die."

She said it like it was a fact, not an opinion.

I laughed again, but it sounded hollow, even to me. Then she smiled once more. "I'm sorry," she said. "It's hard to be around you, that's all." And she was out the door.

I wondered how a few words from a stranger—albeit an intimate stranger—could hurt me as it did, but I spent the night sleeping only fitfully. The next morning dawned gray and bleak and I went through the motions of my day with no zest or energy.

An ugly winter storm closed the airport at the end of the conference I didn't attend, but the good people at the bus company don't let a few inches of snow and ice slow them down. As far as they were concerned, the SEA-PDX corridor was an open and clear straight shot down I-5. I took a taxi to the bus station, not an easy thing in itself given the blizzardy weather (quite rare for Seattle), but my driver negotiated the treacherous roads ably. He deposited me at the station just as the sun was going down, drawing the last meager gray light of the day from the sky like it was nothing but thin ink spilled on the clouds.

I bought my ticket, boarded the coach, and as I searched for a rare empty seat, reflected that if the bus kept to its schedule I should arrive in my home city not much later than if I had taken the plane. What with all the time in getting to the airport, and then security and baggage and so forth, the short flight from the emerald city to the city of roses could sometimes stretch into hours. As for the bus lines, evidently there was not much worry about terrorists blowing up one of their conveyances; security concerns were so small as to cause no delay whatsoever.

Once I got on the bus, I saw that my choices as far as seating arrangements were limited. I vetoed an empty but decidedly uninviting seat next to a mother and her drooling baby, and rejected another adjacent to an obvious drunkard. That left only one empty chair next to a scruffy-looking older man who seemed more than a little interested in me. I stood beside it. He greeted me with the question I quoted at the beginning.

So. It was to be one of those kinds of rides. A fellow traveler on our little planet wanting to get to know me, make a *connection* of some depth. He wished to be a fleeting friend I would never see again, and the whole relationship being so transitory, he hoped that I would reveal something of myself to satisfy his need for a stimulating frisson. Not that I judged him for this need. I had some of my own needs. Or desires, if you prefer. In

any case, I have been a doctor for some years. I have encountered such needs in all manner of person. They are
a secret aspect of numerous lives.

I sat down and cleared my throat. "That's an odd
question," I said. "Do you usually skip over the 'hello,
my name is whatever' part of the social interaction?"

"Depending upon your answer to my question," he
said, "I can engage you in further conversation, or safely
ignore you."

My aisle seat gave me a small advantage, since I
could easily get up and leave, but as I have indicated, I
had no good options for alternative seating so the advantage was moot. In any case, the bus driver had already closed the door and was preparing to embark on
our journey, so even if I wanted to leave the bus itself,
that option was now closed to me if I wanted to maintain any semblance of discretion.

The bus moved slowly backwards, out of its parking place, and presently turned onto a street and before
long we were at top speed on I-5, the tires humming
on bare pavement for some of the time, and plowing
through crunchy ices patches and layers of snow for the
balance. During this embarkation, I sought to distract
myself from my seat mate. I noted that air hissed from

the little round vents on the ceiling above us. Did the filtering system really clean the air, or was I, along with my travel mates, breathing the soup composed of micro-organisms from the breaths of my fellow pilgrims? If only I had attended the conference I was supposed to have attended. Then I might actually *know*.

I continued to study my surroundings, stalling for time, as it were. Next to the vents two lights shone dimly upon us, casting weak shadows and making the whole space between us, between me and this inquisitive man, into some ghastly imitation of a well-lit room. I inserted a finger between my collar and my neck. I felt suddenly warm and confused. This was not my usual milieu and the strangeness of the place took me well out of my comfort zone.

"You didn't even ask *me* the most important question," he said.

"Your name?"

"Ha! No. But call me Grant."

"*Is* that your name?"

"No."

"Then Chuck isn't my name either, but you can call me that."

He studied me for a moment. I studied the back of

the seat in front of me, noted the white patch of material hanging from the top and draped like a bit of curtain. The seat itself was dark gray with scuff marks from the shoes of previous occupants of my seat. I wasn't looking at him, at Grant, but felt him looking at me. A most disconcerting sensation.

He had a demeanor about him of the type that knows he can get what he wants from anyone. He appeared to be the kind of person you want to tell things to. I noted this in the back of my brain and told myself that I would not fall prey to his strength.

"Very good," he said. "You want to play the game."

"Game?"

"The game of life, of deception. The masks and metaphors we use to interact with the world. You've just adopted one. I don't think you have much behind the name, just a vague persona of a bus traveler, or what you think a bus traveler would be like, but still, you dove into the fray. Bravo. You might actually be worth talking to."

"Imagine my joy and rapture. Unconfined."

"Ha again! A sense of humor. Very good. The question you didn't ask is how did I know you were a doctor."

His voice snaked through the air and into my ear like a slithery thing, well-oiled and insistent. It took all of two seconds for me to lose my resolve to resist him. This Grant. "Well," I said. "I barely consider myself a real doctor. I graduated last in my class. And it wasn't a top school by any means. I have little curiosity about the medical profession, or any real desire to improve my skills. I've lost a few patients I shouldn't have. Part of the learning curve, you might say. I should probably not be practicing at all, but I won't voluntarily remove myself from a position that offers abundant respect and plenty of money. Besides, the medical infrastructure has seen to it that I retain my job. Doctors like me, who prescribe pills that the pharmaceutical industry concocts in a myriad of forms and permutations, we're just coasting. I don't ask for your sympathy or even your understanding. I accept any contempt you might feel for me, as my stance is quite contemptible. But, as way of explanation, rather than excuse, you should know that there are many like me. Pill pushers. Doctoring shelters a lot of mediocre talent." I felt, rather than saw, him nod his understanding. I was already an open book to him. I really needed to keep my mouth shut. "Therefore," I continued, "I did not consider it strange that you knew my

profession. I merely assumed you had some kind of ability to search out clues about people."

"I do," he interjected, gently, as if to comment on my
words rather than interrupt or extend them. But I did
not treat his remark as a modifier. Instead I took hold of
myself and slowed way down to the point where I didn't
say anything else for a few seconds. Long enough for
him to pick up his part of the conversation.

"You're a specialist," he said.

I didn't answer. It was not a particularly noteworthy
insight anyway. Most everyone in medicine is a specialist nowadays. I raised my chin, as if to say "wouldn't you
like to know?"

"Oh, come on. You told me a lot already. What's a
little more going to hurt? I'm thinking some kind of der-
matologist maybe. Or plastic surgery. Am I close?"

"Okay," I said, clear irritation in my voice, "how exactly *did* you know I was a doctor?"

"All doctors think they own the world. Haven't you
noticed?"

"You've had a lot of experience with doctors?"

"Some. Every single one I've ever met, they think
their particular superstition, medicine, is the only superstition with any merit."

"I would hardly call medicine superstition."

"Why not? Doctors don't know how to really cure people. Not a single one of you. You try things and hope they work, without ever knowing *why* they work."

"With all possible respect," I said, "I don't think you know what you're talking about."

"And you do, Doctor Last-in-his-class? Are you telling me that you actually had passion for medicine once?"

"Once. You have to or you won't survive medical school. It's a lot of work."

"Even at one of the minor schools?"

"Even there. The work load and the memorization— it's not a minor thing. It takes all of your time and energy."

"So once you graduate and begin practicing, you figure you can kick back and take it easy. You deserve to slack off. Is that it?"

"The one thing I learned from medical school is that the body takes care of itself or it doesn't. We can help along, a little, we in the medical profession, but a lot of what we do is hand holding and hand waving."

"Ah ha!" he said. "Got you. That's just what I said about you doctors not two minutes ago."

I had to admit he was right, and I wondered how I had maneuvered myself into agreeing with him, when, on a fundamental level I most emphatically did *not* agree with him.

I turned my head to see him more clearly. He was in his late fifties. Maybe early sixties. But in that transition age, when youth has given up the fight and wrinkles and grayness begin looking comfortable in their new home. He was a smoker, or had been. A drinker, too. His complexion revealed numerous broken blood vessels and a certain sallow quality that one gets from bathing one's skin in carcinogenic vapors. He sported a beard of sorts, really more like a three or four day stubble that he didn't feel like shaving. His clothes, an old flannel shirt over a yellowing T-shirt, were worn to bare threads in some spots. His jacket was thin and unzipped. Evidently he was not bothered by the cold, or chose to pretend it didn't concern him. I chose not to look at his pants, but felt comfortably assured that they, too, must be old and barely serviceable.

I must have betrayed my distaste. "I see what you're doing," he said. "Trying to put me into my place. The social strata. You're up here—" he put his hand close to the vents "—and I'm down here—" he lowered his hand to chest height "—and that gives you comfort. Knowing I'm one of the lesser thans. But we're all the same, when you come right down to it. No matter what class we are lucky enough to occupy."

"Indeed? Then how about you?" I said. "You ever want to kill someone?"

"Of course, who hasn't? But you have the perfect opportunity for the perfect crime, don't you think?"

"Evidently you think so."

"Well sure. You take a dislike to someone, all you have to do is arrange to have them be your patient. Then you recommend some ghastly surgery, which—surprise!—you are the best one to perform and in the middle of it—oops! A terrible mistake, but he was warned of the risks. Every surgery has risks. Isn't that what you tell all your patients?"

I nodded. "So we are taught in medical school. So experience seems to bear out."

"Well, there you are, then. The perfect crime."

"You forget that I'm a mediocre doctor. No one would believe I was the best at any procedure." This was certainly not true. Doctors have ample opportunity to deceive their patients along these lines. Most people check out a car they intend to buy far more thoroughly than they inquire into the background of their doctors. This small fact has kept many bad doctors in the profession. "Besides," I continued, "it's not so simple to 'arrange' to have someone be a patient. We don't go looking for them. They come to us."

"I'm not saying you should go home and begin advertising for patients to kill."

"Then what are you saying?"

"It's more of a theoretical thing. You can't tell me that such things absolutely don't happen. You can't tell me there isn't at least *one* doctor out there who has done this sort of thing. At least once."

"And your first question, where you asked me if I ever killed a patient, was that a theoretical inquiry as well? Idle curiosity?"

"You don't ride the bus much, do you? Of course not. What doctor rides the bus? No matter what his place in his graduating class."

"What does that have to do with anything?"

Grant shrugged and smiled. "You don't know what happens on these things. People talk. They talk about all kinds of things. You learn a lot about people and what they do, but it helps to break the ice early with something that gets people thinking. Otherwise you end up talking about your grand kids and your dogs. Maybe your childhood."

"And what's wrong with that?"

"Nothing. Except that it's *boring*. For one thing, you don't have any dogs. Or cats. No pets at all, I'd be willing to bet."

That uncomfortable feeling again, like he knew things about me he had no way of knowing. Let alone the *right* to know.

"I keep a cat," I said.

"Ha! No you don't. Liar. Caught you. Nice try, but you're no match for me. Cat owners love the kind of talk we've been having because it's odd, quirky. You are not odd or quirky. Never have been in your life. Your hobbies, if you even have any, are completely normal. Boring. What made you lose your love for medicine?"

An odd question. Again. It made me think. I never had a true love for medicine. It was merely a lucrative profession that I could study for and enter. I had a passion for the wealth medicine could bring me. A lot of doctors are like me in that regard.

"Medicine became dreary," I said.

"When?"

"After medical school. Once I set up my practice. An

endless series of ailing patients. It gets to be a grind after a while. It gets to be a grind very soon, actually."

"All jobs, no matter how glamorous from the outside, are just a series of endless boring duties from the inside. Don't you think so?"

I believe we had a meeting of the minds on that point. "I'm sure," I said.

"Even whoring," he said.

"That's an odd observation. 'Whoring' as you call it, would never be considered a glamorous profession."

"Don't kid yourself, Doc. There's lots of young women who think it would be an exciting way to make a living."

"Ridiculous," I said.

"Oh, really? Do you watch many movies? Glamorous prostitutes are a staple of the form."

"Idle fantasies," I said.

"Fantasies, yes. Idle, no. Movies tell us about the deepest beliefs and desires of the culture. They have to, because their audience is so big. Movies are like a checklist of what the culture cherishes."

"So now you're a social critic."

He shrugged. "I have many talents. Tell me, how much fornicating did you do the last few days? A lot, I bet. And I'll bet double it was with paid partners. Am I right?"

Now thoroughly unnerved, and feeling as though I could never gain an upper hand in our exchange, I determined to shut my mouth and keep it shut. I did not answer his question. Instead I adjusted my collar, pulled my jacket tighter around me and brushed a bit of lint from my knee. I must have presented a comic spectacle to him because he laughed. Not a loud or raucous laugh by any means, just a kind of low volume chuckle, the sort of sound that indicates the owner is in complete control of the situation.

The bus slowed down somewhat. Grant looked outside at the snow falling past the window in long white streaks. Behind the sound of hissing air I heard tinkles of ice particles on the roof.

"We might not make it to Portland tonight," he said.

Was this the sort of boring talk he had wanted to avoid? I didn't know or care. Instead I jumped into the banality of it. "It's nasty out there, that's for sure. I only hope our driver knows what he's doing."

"Even if he doesn't, this is a big vehicle. It can withstand a wreck better than any car. We'd be safe as safe can be. Or at least as safe as we can hope for on a night like this."

I doubted the wisdom behind that statement, but I had no reason to seriously doubt anything Grant told me. I noted the top of his head was balding. His hair hung in a ring on his skull like a fuzzy donut. I had some kind of insight, right there, on the spot, and voiced it without thinking. "You're a clown, aren't you? Or you were one."

He stiffened and I knew I was right. He turned slowly around to face me.

"Tickles was my stage name. The kids loved me."

I felt absurdly proud of myself for my lucky guess. As though I had correctly diagnosed a patient after seeing him for two seconds. Such things occur, but are a rarity. Not the two seconds part. Most doctors make up their minds about what ails a patient within two seconds of meeting them. The correctly part is the rarity.

"'Loved?'" I said. "You don't clown around anymore?"

"It's called *performing*. Not 'clowning around.'"

I raised my hands. "Didn't mean to offend."

He studied me for a second, perhaps trying to discern if I had more such insightful observations. "I retired," he said. "Got sick. Cancer."

"Lung?"

"Throat." He pulled down his collar to show me a scar on his neck.

"Did you think the doctor wanted to kill you?" I asked.

Here he seemed to let his mind drift away, as though he was considering my question with great solemnity. The bus, I noted, was going much slower than normal. Though I did not like the snail's pace, I did appreciate the caution. Better to get to Portland late than not at all.

"She made me stop smoking," said Tickles the Clown. "After she cut into me and took out the tumor. She said if I didn't stop, the next knife would be handled by whoever had the honor of autopsying me. I went to a gig the next week, but my voice was still bad. The kids got scared. Also, I wasn't funny. Never wanted to be funny again. I could tell. The cancer ate up all the funny I had in me. Every last bit of it. Worse, the kids could tell. You can't fool them. Also the parents. It was a birthday party. I stopped the show early and gave them back their money. Haven't performed since."

"How long ago was that?"

"Two years."

"Were you good?"

He shook his head. "I was okay. Never the best. If I actually went to a clown school I probably would have finished last in my class. Like you."

"So," I said. "We're brothers under the skin."

"Yeah."

"Ever want to kill any of your audience?"

"My audience was *children*."

I nodded. "Ever want to kill any of them? I've met a few kids I wouldn't mind seeing gone. As in never existed."

"Don't be sick," he said.

I laughed. "Just trying to get to know you," I said. "Trying to talk about things that aren't boring."

"Okay," he said. "I get what you're doing. Trying to turn around what I said to you so it sticks to me."

"Something like that."

As we talked, and as the bus slowed even more, I noticed that we didn't always maintain a straight path on the highway. We slid a couple of times. Nothing dramatic, but enough to notice. Some of the other passengers also noticed. They reacted with short cries. It wasn't a universal reaction; some passengers were asleep, and they were not roused from their slumbers. Nevertheless an air of tension began to permeate the bus, as though we were all waiting for a terrible mishap to occur at any moment.

For myself, I knew the possibility was strong. The ice falling on our roof became even more insistent. It seemed clear that if it was pummeling our roof, it must also be coating the roadway. Tickles the Clown felt it as well. "I don't know about this bus ride," he said.

The words barely left his mouth when the intercom crackled into annoying static and the voice of the driver, scarcely audible under the sandpapered air, informed us that we were going to take an unscheduled stop at the next rest area, only a few miles distant. I did not know just how tense I had been, but his words relaxed me immediately. I felt my shoulders slump and a smile crossed Tickles the Clown's lips. "Thank God for that," he said. "I was starting to get worried."

I reflected that it would have been better for me to have remained in Seattle, but what good did such thoughts do me? I was not in Seattle. I was on this bus.

Neither of us spoke for the next few minutes. Tickles the Clown stared out the window. "Getting real icy out there," he said. I tried to look out as well, positioning myself to view a corner of the window next to his head. I saw a couple of cars had slid off the road onto the shoulder where their emergency flashing lights blinked dimly through the fog of the falling precipitation, which now appeared to be a hardy mix of snow, ice, sleet, and who knew what else. Other cars, I noted, had slid completely off the shoulder and were peacefully resting in the median separating our southbound lanes from the northbound lanes. Dim figures seemed to wander around the vehicles, like ghostly zombies in the night, dazed and blind.

I wondered how we were maintaining our trajectory on the slick surface. I-5 had become a skating rink. The bus could not have been going more than five miles an hour when we finally, and gingerly, so it seemed, entered the ramp to the rest area. The bus curved around in a stately and careful manner, like a tipsy queen approaching her throne, and finally halted in an extended parking area, next to several semi trucks. The parking lot was already almost filled to capacity. Many people evidently had the same idea, which was to save themselves by seeking sanctuary here.

The driver's voice crackled over the intercom again. "Folks," he said, "we're going to rest here for a while until the roads clear up. There's vending machines here and some hot coffee if you want it. We'll get under way again as soon as it's safe to do so."

I sighed and leaned my head back on my chair.

"You need to call anyone?" said Tickles the Clown. "Anyone need to know you're going to be late?"

I turned my head toward him. "You should know that," I said. "You're insight man, aren't you? You know what makes people laugh because you know their secrets. Isn't that how it works?"

"Something like that, but not exactly. You're single, that's for sure. No wife would have you, the way you fool around with working girls, but I was thinking of your office. You have an office, don't you?"

Up to that point, despite myself, I had found Tickles the Clown at least a little interesting, but now that we were in a dreary interstate rest area, with no indication of when we might leave it, his incessant questions no longer intrigued me on any level.

"I need to pee," I said, and got up to join the throng of passengers leaving the bus. We shuffled along the aisle like old people who had misplaced their walkers. I thought about Tickles the Clown's question. It seemed to prey on my mind far more than it had any right to. I never wanted to kill a patient. Never. So why did his question trouble me? It sent my mind along paths I was unaccustomed to traveling. I did not know how to be in that forbidding country, that place where hidden motives are made manifest.

The line moved particularly slowly, much more slowly than seemed normal. When I finally got to the head of the line and descended the steps at the door, I saw why: the parking lot was slick as a polished stone, and my fellow passengers found it necessary to hang onto the bus for a few seconds to get themselves as situated as possible before embarking on the trek across the parking lot to the restrooms and the machines dispensing poisonous snacks in wretched plastic bags.

I myself stepped very gingerly off the bus and allowed my feet to acclimate to the slippery surface before pushing away. I did not take steps. Instead I slid my shoes along the ice. Sharp drops of cold rain pelted my head and shoulders. Some of them coalesced on my jacket sleeve into crusty bits of frost. The drops that made it to the ground froze instantly. This precipitation could go on for hours. We could all be here for a long time. I made my slow way to the restrooms, where I joined a small line. Even in the cold, an unpleasant odor came from the direction of the restroom, a ghastly mixture of acrid cleaning solutions, body odor, and human waste. Suddenly the interior of the bus seemed more than a little inviting, despite my seat mate.

I felt a tap on my shoulder. I turned around. A young man, no more than twenty, smiled at me.

"Yes?" I said.

"You just came off the bus," he said.

"What of it?"

"That bus isn't going anywhere the rest of the night. I've got a four by four with chains. I can drive through anything. You want a ride to Portland? Two hundred dollars cash. In advance."

The term "highway robbery" seemed the most appropriate under the circumstances and I almost accused him of indulging in just such a crime but managed to hold my tongue.

I had a bag on the bus, but there was nothing in it that I truly needed.

"Let's go," I said. "Where's your vehicle?"

"In advance," he said, and put out his hand.

"I'll give you the money after I see your rig."

He seemed doubtful, then shrugged and grabbed my sleeve. I did not pull away. Something about his sturdy youth made me want to lean on him a little. We slid and shuffled on the sidewalk across the rest area to where the passenger cars were parked and came to an impressive and imposing vehicle that gave me confidence immediately. It was square and heavy with big wide tires fitted with thick chains.

"Do these work in ice?" I said, indicating the chains with my foot.

"They have spikes on them."

I leaned down and examined one of the links. There were indeed tiny but lethal looking claws on the chain.

"Impressive," I said.

"They're illegal," he said. "Tears up the road. But what do I care? Or you?"

Indeed. What did I care? I reached into my pocket and peeled off ten twenties from my billfold and handed them to him. He took the money with a grin, opened the back door, and I climbed in. I expected him to get into the driver's seat immediately, completely missing the point of his enterprise. He tapped on the window and I rolled it down. "Yes?"

"You sit tight for a few minutes. I'm going to round up a couple more."

"Couple more?"

"You don't expect me to drive with two seats empty, do you? That's like throwing away four hundred bucks."

He thumped the side of his vehicle and turned and slid back towards the restrooms. I had no doubt that he would find two other passengers, but I didn't want to wait. I wanted this dreary journey to end, soon.

I watched him go back to the restroom and try to cajole more passengers into his vehicle, apparently with little luck. He went down the line and everyone refused him. That made me a little nervous. Did they know something I didn't?

While I waited I examined my surroundings. The vehicle, a Humvee, was relatively new. It was roomy as hell and I felt the sturdiness of its construction. I would trust this vehicle anywhere, anytime. I decided to relax and wait patiently for my savior to return.

Before long a dark shape approached from behind. I noted that he had no sliding companions, so assumed he could not find anymore willing to take his offer. The driver's door swung open and who should slide in behind the steering wheel but my old pal Tickles the Clown. He turned around and grinned at me. "Hey, buddy," he said.

I would have expected my reaction to be less than accommodating, but I liked the idea of Tickles the Clown and me sharing the same vehicle again. I reflected, on the spot, that perhaps I was rather more disturbed than I had given myself credit for.

"Long time," I said.

"Not long enough, though, huh?"

"He convinced you to cough up two hundred dollars?" I said.

"Who?"

"The owner of this vehicle. Aren't you going to Portland with me?"

"That wasn't the plan, but hey—" he looked down next to the steering column. "Lookee here. Keys." He turned around and grinned at me. "I've always wanted to drive one of these things."

He started the engine and before I could say a word, certainly before I could exit the vehicle, we were off in a stolen Humvee.

"You want to stop for anyone?" said Tickles the Clown.

I hesitated. A dose of adrenaline had elevated my senses. I found that I was enjoying the thought of riding to Portland with Tickles the Clown. I mentally shook my head, as though attempting to shake the craziness out of myself. "No," I said. "Let's not stop for anyone."

I saw the truck's owner in the distance on the island

between the parking lots. Getting his vehicle stolen was no less than he deserved. As far as I was concerned, anyway.

"You're not half bad, Doc," said Tickles the Clown. I felt, rather than saw the grin on his face. I imagined wide clown lips, bright red. The thought gave me a warm feeling inside, something I was not accustomed to. It alarmed me for a moment, then I decided it was not necessarily a bad thing.

As we entered the ramp that would take us back onto the highway, I saw the young man do a double take in our direction, then observed him slipping and sliding over the ice, arms flailing, in severe danger of upending himself, and I felt great satisfaction. I laughed out loud, a snorting kind of laugh, derisive in its explosiveness.

"Ha!" said Tickles the Clown. "You're having fun, aren't you?"

"Yes," I said, admitting it to myself as much as to him.

"You know this isn't going to end well, right? We're stealing a particularly expensive vehicle."

"No 'we' involved at all," I said. "You're the thief. I was coerced into this. An innocent victim."

"Oh, Doc! You hurt me to the core. I thought we

were in this together. Buddies to the end."

"Buddies until the end. Then you're on your own."

"You're cold, Doc. Way colder than I thought you would be."

"You already knew I was not a model humanitarian."

"You got me there, Doc."

I never particularly liked it when patients called me Doc. It always seemed too casual and familiar. I was a professional, albeit a mediocre one, and should be treated with respect and addressed with some formality. "Doc" fell short on both counts. Now, with Tickles the Clown repeatedly using the designation, I found it all the more irritating. "Don't call me Doc," I said.

"Oops," he said. "That a sore point, or something? You want to tell me your real name, then?"

"I told you, it's Chuck. Call me Chuck."

"Funny. If you're anything, you're a Charles."

He had a point.

"Just stick to Chuck."

He put his hand up and waved it around as though he were tossing a butterfly into the air. "As you wish."

We were practically the only vehicle on the road. I saw some red tail lights far in the distance ahead of us and a couple of headlights far far behind us. Tickles the

Clown had the Humvee situated on the left side of the lane. Our tires seemed to grind up the ice like an ice pick on steroids. I felt the chains bumping under us, as though we were going over an endless series of potholes. A very satisfying feeling to be on a stable rig in these conditions.

"Do you have a story ready for the officer when we get stopped?" I said.

"That's your department. I'm just a sick clown. You have the college education. Right now, I've got to concentrate on the road and the driving."

We remained squarely on the road, going straight and true. No sliding. I could not escape the thought that this was a beautiful thing, a wondrous thing.

"That guy's going to call the police," I said.

"He's got illegal equipment on this rig." So Tickles the Clown had noticed the chains. "He's going to be due for a heavy fine."

"Still," I said. "Better to pay the fine and get his vehicle back. This isn't an economy car by any means."

"He's going to think about it for a while, though. Besides, the police have other things to do tonight besides tracking down some rich prick's Humvee. They have a lot of wrecks to deal with."

"You know the priorities of the police?"

He shrugged. "Just a guess. Probably a good one though."

I could easily, if stopped, claim that I was fooled into going along with Tickles the Clown because I thought he was the owner of the vehicle. The young man was just someone rounding up rides. That respect I mentioned earlier goes a long way when it comes to dealing with the authorities. They would believe me much more readily than they would believe a cancerous clown, to put it as crudely and clearly as possible.

"You seem to be handling this vehicle just fine."

"Uh huh. That's not a problem. But you could be right. It might be a minor miracle if we make it to Portland unmolested by any of the cops along the way."

"What made you want to do this?"

"I'm trying to save your life," he said.

"That's what doctors do. Not clowns."

"Says you. Doctors only make you well. Clowns make you laugh. If you're laughing, you don't need to be well. Laughter will save your life every time that doctors will let you down. Don't forget that. And what are you doing back there? Come up front and sit with me. I could use the company."

Reluctantly I climbed over the back of the seat and slid into the passenger seat. The windshield wipers were making a valiant attempt at scraping away the ice, but it was beginning to build up around the edges and slowly creeping towards the center of the glass.

"Anything you can do about the visibility issue?" I asked.

"I've got the defogger on full blast. You have any suggestions?"

I didn't. I turned on the radio. A country station spewed out some lyrics about a lonely man on his ranch trying to impress a woman. "Anything you want to hear?" I said.

"That sounds fine to me," he said.

"Seriously?"

"Sure. You don't like it?"

"Seems kind of boring, don't you think? Weren't you the one who didn't like boring? I mean, really, some lovesick cowboy wailing about how he can't have the woman he loves."

"I don't pay attention to the words much. It's just a mask for the music."

"Well I'm not crazy about the music, either."

"Then pick something *you* like."

I punched buttons until a jazz station sent some smoky riffs through the cab of the Humvee. I have never been particularly enamored with jazz, but it seemed the appropriate soundtrack to our road trip: trippingly eclectic and meandering, like insecure people trying to find a purchase on the world and failing miserably.

"How are you with that?" I asked.

"It'll do for a while," said Tickles the Clown.

"How long were you a clown?" I said.

"Twenty years."

"That's a lot of invested time to give up on."

He shrugged. "Things change. Nothing lasts forever." He paused. "Sure wish I still smoked. Now would be a great time for some cigarettes. Don't you think?"

"I never smoked."

"Too bad. You don't know what you're missing. I still think about taking in a deep lungful of the stuff. It's like you're playing with fire. With death. Stuff that could kill you but you survive."

He was obviously forgetting the scar on his neck. "But you quit. On the advice of a member of the superstitious clan."

"You mean my doctor?"

"Of course your doctor. Who else would I be talking

about?"

"Every time before a performance, I'd make sure I smoked a whole cigarette. It wasn't always easy. People have this phobia about smoke. They made me step outside. Which was okay, I guess, but sometimes it was cold and wet. Sometimes they didn't like that a clown, who's supposed to be kid-friendly, smoked. Bad example and all that."

"They might have had a point."

"Listen, I worked hard for those kids. I always put on a good show. Not every moment of my life had to be an *example* for kids. We don't live for kids, you know."

Ahead of us the lights of Olympia began to brighten the sky, the dull illumination fighting through the muck of the precipitation. I thought that perhaps some of the rain was letting up, just a little. Tickles the Clown seemed to notice it too, or else we shared the same delusion. "Weather is starting to improve," he said. "A little."

I wondered if we were going to make it through Olympia. Surely the local police knew of the stolen Humvee by now.

"I got some friends in this town," he said.

"Clown friends?"

"You trying to be funny?"

"No. I was just asking."

Our expedition had suddenly taken on a decidedly sour feeling, like the joy had leaked out of us. Not ten minutes ago I felt as adventurous as any frontier-traversing pioneer. Now I felt shamed by my participation in our escapade, and shame was not a big part of my emotional makeup. Never had been. I kept it to a bare minimum, just enough to function in society to my specifications.

"As it happens, I do know some fellow performers here."

"Ah."

"In fact. I'm thinking we should drop in on them. What do you say?"

"That wasn't the plan," I said.

"Plan?" He cupped his hand around his ear and leaned toward me. "I never heard any plan," he said. "You mention a *plan*? Because if you did, it got by me."

Then he looked at me and laughed. I pondered that laugh for some seconds. It was a decidedly harsh sound, perhaps even hostile. He was evidently not the variety of clown which is always upbeat and fun. He was a clown with *depth* of feeling, and harbored a dark side to his personality.

He had a point, though. I assumed we were going to Portland, but we never agreed to such a course of action, and so, if he wanted to detour into the environs of greater Olympia, who was I to object?

"These friends of yours," I said. "What would they think of a fornicating pediatrician?"

"Pediatrician? You take care of children?"

"Yes, as a matter of fact."

"Ha! Double fucking *ha*! I can't believe it. You hate children."

"An over statement. I don't hate them. I merely prefer not to be around them except on a professional basis."

"The parents of these children, do they know about your private life?"

"No. Why should they?"

"Well, you know about their private life, don't you?"

A question with barbs, that one. Daring me again, as was his way.

"I take personal histories, of course. But I don't pry into things that are not my business."

He snorted. I saw his hand fumble towards his shirt pocket, as if he were looking for something. Perhaps his cigarettes, still there in his mind, like a phantom limb.

Then he dropped his hand and seemed to refocus his attention on the road ahead. "Exit coming up," he said.

Green signs, coated with ice, flicked by us. The defroster seemed to have won the battle with the ice and the windshield afforded us a panoramic view of the conditions ahead. It did not seem to me that things were any better. Visibility was less than a quarter mile. The part I could see was streaked with icy trails like a million shooting stars, illuminated by our headlights. I had thought the weather was improving, but evidently that was premature. The precipitation maintained its intensity. In fact, it seemed to be whipping up even more of a frenzy. It gave our reality a kind of painterly aspect, as though we were traveling through pure motion, carried along, as I fancied, upon some ethereal artist's imagination. I am not much given to thoughts of wild visions like this, but the night invited me along unfamiliar pathways and I, apparently, wished to answer the invitation.

The Humvee slowed way down, enough to allow a single vehicle to pass us, gingerly, and with wide berth, on our left. I glimpsed a driver grimly hunched over her steering wheel, eyes wide and frightened. I found myself hoping she was going to make it home, or wherever she had to be, safely. I *never* had such thoughts. It puzzled me that I should be plagued by them now. What good did it do me to worry about a stranger's well being?

We could have been outrun by a snail as we slowed to a crawl on the curved ramp. Tickles the Clown seemed to know what he was doing. "This isn't the usual exit I take," he said. "But it's probably better to get off the expressway, don't you think?"

I gave no answer, having no particular insight into the best path we should be taking.

The road straightened out, ended at a set of lights, which displayed green for us, and we went through without slowing any further. We were soon going down a street lined with the sorts of businesses that display tall garish signs by the road: gas stations, convenience stores, and such. No other vehicles were on the road.

"I love it when a town shuts down like this," said Tickles the Clown.

"There's a certain tranquility to it," I said in as agreeable a manner as I could.

"You ever mix business with pleasure?" he said.

"What do you mean?"

"These parents that bring you their sick kids. It's usually the mother, I bet. Right?"

"Yes, that's true."

"You ever, you know—" he closed his fist and made a pumping gesture toward the windshield several times, mimicking a decidedly graceful harmonic motion "—give it to the mother?"

"Never have. That would be decidedly unprofessional."

"What? Why? You take care of the kid, then take care of the mother on your own time. What's the unprofessional part?"

"If I have to explain—"

He waved his hand. "Yeah, yeah. You're still all high and mighty and looking down on me. I get it. But see, I'm just living life the way it's lived. I'm not hiding behind anything like 'professional ethics' or whatever you call it."

"It's not hiding. It's an important part of the profession."

"A profession you don't even care about."

"That's not true. I care about the profession of medicine. I just find it difficult to motivate myself to becoming an exemplary practitioner of it."

He snorted. As well he should. Even to myself that statement sounded ridiculous. I sought to divert the conversation away from my character flaws. "And what about you?" I said. "Does clowning have ethics? Did you ever get involved with the mothers who hired you for their kid's birthday parties?"

"I really wanted to. Lots of times. But I showed up to my gigs in costume. Women don't want to fuck a clown."

It sounded like the most pathetic thing I had heard in a long time. "I suspect even more so when the occasion is the birthday of their child," I said.

"You know," he said, "I don't think that would have mattered."

"If you think that, I don't think you understand mothers."

"And you do?"

"I didn't say that."

"I bet I helped a lot more kids that you ever have. Or ever will."

I chose not to engage him on that subject. He had his delusions, which seemed to give him comfort. Who was I to point out that he was not humanity's savior? Was it my place to inform him of the fact that *clowns,* of all things, did not help humanity nearly as much as he thought they did? A clown, or any performing amusement for that matter, at *best,* was nothing more than a temporary diversion. Good for a laugh or two, but it could never go beyond that to anything truly beneficial. Nothing like what a doctor could do.

"You could be right," I said.

He heard the deception in my voice. How could it be otherwise? It was a completely bald-faced lie I just told him. "You're so full of shit," he said, "your eyes are brown."

"I haven't heard that particular idiom since I was in grade school."

"I know them all," he said. "Performers like me, who worked in comedy, we had to know all those sayings because the kids knew them. You have to be smarter than the kids, otherwise they don't pay any attention to you. They think you're nothing."

"Surely an overstatement," I said.

"And by the way," he said, "we have ethics. I did."

"I don't doubt it."

He glanced at me and tried to decide if I was mocking him. I wasn't quite sure myself and he looked away quickly. His face turned a subtle shade of red. Was that rage beginning to surface? Was I in some danger? We traveled in silence for a mile or so. Ice continued to coat the roads. I saw ice encasing buildings, glazing the roofs and walls with a translucence that reminded me of jelly or smoked glass. Ice also covered most of the road signs to a depth of what looked like a quarter to half an inch. Ice sat on top of power lines like silver snakes. Many of them were bound to collapse, which meant there were going to be power outages all over the region.

"Hey," said Tickles the Clown. "There's a convenience store open." He slowed even more until the crunch of the chains came to a merciful stop and I realized we had been shouting at each other over the chewing chains and the breaking ice. He surveyed the area, then drove past the store to the empty parking lot of a real estate agent's office, where he pulled in behind, away from view of the street, and stopped the Humvee and turned off the engine. The jazz, which had become a little annoying, died with the motor. The pinging sound of freezing rain took up the musical accompaniment to our journey with an atonal and interminable refrain. I was now thoroughly sick of the weather.

"I thought we were going to the store," I said.

"We're ditching this beast. It's been a fun ride, but we shouldn't push our luck, wouldn't you say?"

"This vehicle is our only shelter."

"Ha! Shelter. I heard a wise man once say the only

roof he needed was the sky."

"Such a man did not live in the Pacific Northwest in the wintertime."

"Comedian, huh? Well, you're not making me laugh. Come on to the store with me. I need your money." He grinned.

He was right that it was probably best to abandon the Humvee, and I was not a little relieved that we were no longer going to be associated with it, but there was still the matter of the weather and our less than optimal shelter from it.

But he had no interest in such musings. He stepped out of the car and crunched around to the back, where he opened the rear and began rummaging around in the various piles of clothes and tools and such items as tend to accumulate in vehicles. I turned around in my seat. "What are you looking for?" I said.

"Something to cut those chains," he said. "Get out of the car, now, please. The next leg of our journey is about to begin."

I turned back around to face the windshield which was already beginning to cake up with ice, now that the wipers were stilled. I sighed and opened the door and stepped outside. Icy pinpricks immediately pelted my face and the top of my head. I hiked my jacket up over my head to afford some protection, but it was slight. The cold air seemed to find every seam in my clothing and insert icicles through them. I stepped carefully over the ice-covered pavement until I stood next to Tickles the Clown. He had found a pair of pliers and held them up proudly. "This will do nicely," he said. I, already miserable far beyond what I was normally used to, said nothing as he crouched next to the rear tire of the Humvee, inserted the pliers between the chain and the tire wall, and used the cutting edges deep in the vee of the pliers's arms to sever the wire-like links of the chains. He worked rapidly and efficiently, pulling off lengths of the chain and handing them up to me. I dutifully took them in my hands, which were already half numb with cold. I noted the hooks on the lengths of the wires. They were somewhat dulled, probably by our recent travels, but still appeared to have a good point to them, as though they could be used to inflict severe damage to someone.

"You aren't thinking of robbing that store, are you?" I said.

He gave me a how-could-you-be-so-stupid? look and I felt immediately chagrined.

"Sorry," I mumbled, probably not quite loud enough

for him to hear.

When he had pulled off several lengths, he stood up and took them from me. "Sit down," he said.

I sat on the end of the open space of the Humvee and with impatient waving gestures of his hands he indicated that I should raise my leg. I did so and he wrapped three lengths of the chains around my shoe and secured them in place by twisting the ends with the pliers, like securing a twist tie around a plastic bag. He continued the procedure on my other shoe, and then he sat down and handed me the pliers. "Your turn," he said.

My hands were now so numb that I could barely feel the pliers against my skin, but I stood and he raised his foot and I tried to perform the same actions he had just accomplished. I succeeded, after a fashion, but had to admit my handiwork did not look as smart and finished as his. He didn't seem to care. He stood up and chucked me in the shoulder with his fist, gently, a kind of friendly winking jab, and thumped me on the back. "This will get us through the ice," he said. "You'll see." He leaned close to me so I could smell his breath, even in the cold and wet.

The precipitation may have slacked off, I was no longer sure. Even if it did, now that I was in it, instead of sheltered from it in the Humvee, I decided it didn't matter if the severity of the storm was marginally less or more from minute to minute. It would feel miserable no matter what. And I was about as miserable as I could feel right then. I had it in mind to get back in the Humvee, police be damned. I welcomed the thought of a jail cell for the night. At least it would be dry and warm. Certainly warmer than I was feeling now.

Tickles the Clown took one step forward on the ice, back toward the road. "Hey," he said. "It works. I feel like I'm never going to fall!"

I sighed and turned toward him and extended a foot of my own. He was right. A feeling of security overwhelmed me immediately. The spikes dug into the ice and secured my foot in place as though it had been nailed there to the parking lot. He pulled a backpack from the vehicle and slung it over one shoulder. "He won't mind that we took this," said Tickles the Clown. "He'll be happy he got his precious truck back." I thought he was probably right about that. Then he tossed the keys back into the Humvee and closed the back.

"You going to call someone and tell them where the rig is?" I asked.

"Someone will figure it out. After the storm is over."

He looked up at the sky, as though he might see something of interest, but there was nothing there except blackness coursed with streaks of gray. He grabbed my arm and pushed me toward the store we had passed earlier.

After we got walking for a couple of minutes, it didn't seem so bad outside. My body heat began to warm me. Not much, but enough that I could tell myself I wasn't going to die.

"We need to bring something to the party," said Tickles the Clown.

"Party?"

"Well sure. This is the perfect night for it, don't you think? Where else you going to go?"

"Where's the party?"

"Not too far. I ditched here so we wouldn't have a long way to walk."

I didn't like his evasiveness but I was afraid to ask for specifics. Was it half a mile? Ten miles?

We arrived at the storefront. Impossible bright light spilled into the parking lot, but I had the feeling it was fighting a losing battle against the storm. The place should have seemed like an oasis. Instead it looked sad.

It wanted to be a mushroom growing in a cesspool but definitely looked more like it was going to drown in the muck. I half expected the lights to flicker and blink out.

We stepped inside, Tickles the Clown first, me following. I carried an air of resignation I found peculiar and alarming. I was not one to follow anyone, and yet, here I was, following this—clown. A clown who seemed to know something about what to do when civilization begins to strain at itself.

The store held lots of snack items: candy bars, chips, donuts, and such. Also two big aisles of beverages, tending to the carbonated sugary end of the spectrum, although several sections of the cooler held beer of various brands and potencies. One aisle in the back appeared to display items resembling real food: canned soup, packets of dry beans and rice. Piles of frozen dinners next to the beer winked at us, as though inviting our participation in their debauchery.

The clerk, a young man with close cut locks and numerous bits of metal adorning his ears, lips, eyebrows, and tongue, smiled at us in a mechanical way.

"Hey," said Tickles the Clown. "Keeping warm and dry?"

"Trying. Don't look forward to walking home."

I wanted to tell him to go to the Humvee parked a couple of buildings down and make himself a pair of ice walkers, but refrained.

"Glad you're open." I said.

"You're lucky. The boss told me to close early. No business. You're the first ones I've seen in two hours. I'll be closing up in about fifteen minutes."

I looked at my watch. A quarter to nine.

"We'll be quick," said Tickles the Clown. "Just need to get a few things."

We walked to the back of the store, our newly forged hardware clicking on the floor like we were overgrown dogs with unclipped toenails. Tickles the Clown grabbed up bags of corn and potato chips and tucked them under his arms. "You like beer?" he asked.

"Occasionally. But I want something hot, not cold tonight."

"I hear you," he said. "No beer."

I stepped a few feet away from him and found a section of nuts and dried fruit. I selected a few bags and tucked them under my arms.

"We could be buying for the apocalypse," he said.

"What?"

"The world could be ending, you know. We need to

choose wisely."

The world could be ending? "It's just an ice storm," I said.

"How long have you been living in the Northwest?"

"Long enough."

"Oh come on. Tell me. Aren't we past the time of secrets? If you've lived here enough years, you know this storm is going on a lot longer than it should."

I didn't think we were past any secrets, but his irritation alarmed me. "Tell you what," I said. "Why don't you go on to your party, or whatever it is, without me. We don't need each other. We passed a hotel a short distance back. I'm going to get a room for the night and find my way back home tomorrow."

His eyes darkened. He wouldn't look at me. I wanted him to. I thought that would mean he was not too angry with me, but I could see he had a large reservoir of anger and had been saving it up for just such an occasion as this: his traveling companion daring to assert his own independence.

"If that's the way you want it," he said. "I thought we were having fun."

"Your act must have been somewhat peculiar if you think of this as fun," I said.

"That some kind of crack? You seem to like bad-mouthing my profession. How would you like it if I told some doctor jokes?"

"Do you know any? You use any in your act?"

"Guy says to his doctor, 'Doc, it hurts when I do this.' Doctors says 'Don't do that.'"

Was I supposed to laugh? Groan? What?

"Or this one," he said. "Doctor tells a guy he's got *cancer*. Guys says I want a second opinion. Doctor says 'Okay, you're ugly, too.'"

Again, was I expected to have a reaction? Did something like this actually happen to him?

"Look," I said, "I'm sorry you got cancer."

"You think it's my smoking, don't you?"

"You smoked. You got throat cancer. If I was a gambling man, that's where I'd put my money. No offense."

"You know there's this gas called radon, right? It's everywhere. In the ground. It gives people cancer."

I shrugged. "Okay. You got throat cancer from radon. Was that the second opinion you wanted?"

"They used to tell people to smoke. Said it was good for us."

"That was a long time ago. Anyway, what's your current prognosis?"

"I don't know."

"What do you mean? What do your tests say?"

"I haven't been back since the surgery and the chemo."

"That's fucking stupid, you know. You know that, right? You need to follow up on your treatment."

"That what they teach you in that crappy medical school you went to?"

"You don't have to go to medical school to know that. Anyone will tell you. A five-year-old knows that much."

"What do you know about kids?"

"I treat them, remember."

"I entertained them, remember? I know a *lot* more than you ever will."

He was bitter about his disease. I didn't blame him. I sure never wanted cancer. I've seen kids with cancer and it is always terrible. Hardened my heart considerably, just to protect myself from the pain of it. From the ridiculous deity who deemed it necessary to make a child suffer. I'm always happy to send them onto an oncologist and get them out of my office and my life. I always send them to the best, I don't just shuffle them off onto someone with skills no better than my own. I do care, in my way. I care enough to help them find someone who can truly help them. Maybe Tickles the Clown had a point, though. Maybe he really did help kids more than I ever did. Doctors hear it all the time: Laughter is the best medicine. It's not true. Not in any sense that matters. Cancer cells don't care if you watch a funny movie and wet your pants and split your sides, they just go on merrily reproducing.

I wondered if Tickles the Clown ever entertained truly ill children. I knew some hospitals brought in clowns and other such performers for the sick kids. I actually thought it was a good idea, but I never kidded myself that it ever arrested their conditions. It was just something to make them feel better for a little while. Break up the hell of being in a hospital.

"Figuring me out, huh?" said Tickles the Clown.

"What?" I climbed out of my musings, aware that I had drifted away. Such an action was a feature of my personality I tried to hide from others, with varying degrees of success.

"I see you," he said. "You're always off somewhere. Bet your patients hate it."

"None of them mention it."

"Because they know it won't do any good. Kids size

you up pretty quick, you know. They've got you figured out in two seconds."

I laughed.

"What's so funny?"

I didn't tell him that doctors did the exact same thing. "How about you?" I said. "You figure out your audience in two seconds?"

He ignored me and went back to collecting foodstuffs. I realized I still thought of him as a clown. A *working* clown, while he saw that part of his life as over, even maybe a little tragic. After all, he was a performer. Over the top was his bread and butter wasn't it? No call for subtlety in his profession.

"Hey," said the clerk. "You guys about done? I wanna close up and get out of here."

Tickles the Clown thumped me on the chest. "Let's get our shit and amscray."

Pig Latin. I rolled my eyes, but got down to business. I went to the front of the store where a cooler held some pre-made sandwiches which looked semi edible. I grabbed two of them and put them on the counter with my bags of nuts and raisins, figuring these would get me through the night to the morning. Tickles the Clown deposited his findings next to mine and the clerk began ringing up our purchases. As he scanned each item, Tickles the Clown stuffed it into his backpack. When he got to one of mine, I put up my hand and shook my head. He hesitated, but left my sandwiches and bags on the counter. The clerk announced the total. I gave him a couple of twenty dollar bills and told him to keep the change for his trouble.

His eyes brightened immediately and he put my purchases into a plastic bag and handed it to me.

"Be careful getting home," I said.

"I will," he answered and his eyes urged us to the exit. I put my arm around Tickles the Clown's shoulder and we click-clacked our way outside, where the nastiness was still coming down. The lock latched shut behind us and the lights of the store dimmed a few seconds later. We remained near the door, where an overhang protected us from most of the moisture.

"Have fun with your friends," I said.

"Yeah," he said. "Have fun with yourself, I guess. Probably no streetwalkers out tonight. Too bad. They could probably do some good business on a night like this. Lonely kind of weather, you know."

"I expect to be asleep within the hour."

"You even sure they have a vacancy at that motel?"

"If they don't, I'll sleep in the lobby."

"Well," he said. "I think you might be kind of a dick, but I'm not sure. Maybe you're okay. Thing is, it's been a little bit fun, hasn't it? Your adventure with the clown. You going to tell your friends about it when you get home? If you have any friends, which I'm not exactly sure you do. I'm your friend now. I guess I was always your friend, we just didn't know it. We just had to find each other, you know?"

"And find each other we did," I said. "And now we must part. I bid you Godspeed on your journey. All your journeys."

With that, I turned from him and began walking along the icy sidewalk, glad to be rid of him, but also glad that I still had the contraption he had devised for me. I regretted being a party to the theft of the vehicle, but not too much. The young man would be reunited with his love object in due course and all would be well, except that he would be shorted some income for the day, which was not my concern.

The street lights along my way contrived to illumi-nate the air over me, but they were not having the best time of it. Mostly they highlighted the streaks of rain. The air had gotten a few degrees warmer, so it was just rain now, but the ground and the power lines were still cold, so that meant the rain turned to ice as soon as it contacted anything solid. Which meant the ice was still building up. Probably be another day before any of it started melting. If it was clear tomorrow, the sun would thaw it out by afternoon. I hoped. Then I would have to find another way to Portland. Probably rent a car.

Not a single vehicle was on the road. The landscape I traversed seemed as desolate as Antarctica, and at least as forbidding.

I saw the parking lot of the motel was completely full. Probably the vehicles of smart people who got off the interstate hours ago, before it got so treacherous. As I approached, the VACANCY sign flicked off and on two times, then the NO to the left of the V came on and I saw the light at the front of the store go off. I hurried my pace as best I could in my makeshift crampons, and arrived at the door within a few seconds and found myself banging my fist repeatedly on it, trying to gain the attention of the person who just turned out the lights.

I was scared being out there. I felt a most peculiar sensation in my belly, as though I had just been told I was going to die. The back of my head shivered and this set off a kind of chain reaction throughout my body so that before long I was shaking with fear and my teeth were chattering.

I must have been out there for a good four or five minutes, which seemed closer to four or five days, before I heard footsteps, muffled, but regular, coming toward the door. I tried to compose myself before the door opened, but failed miserably. When the door finally opened, and revealed a middle-aged woman, stout and matronly, with her hands on her hips, and a disapproving expression on her face, as though she were my mother fussing over my state, I stepped forward and heard a high-pitched voice, my own, say "Please let me in, I'm so cold." The entire sentence was punctuated by my teeth sliding one against the other in a mad dance that needed only a dirge-like organ accompaniment to complete my feeling that my own death was imminent.

"You look like a wet cat," she said. She put out her hand and grabbed me by the wrist and pulled me inside. My chains dug into the carpeting of her floor and I nearly stumbled forward, but she caught me. "Easy, there," she said.

I stood up straight and took in my surroundings. I was in a decidedly dreary and dilapidated room. One chair in the corner. A worn desk to one side. A table with piles of brochures extolling the recreational opportunities abounding in this area, and an odor of mustiness pervading everything. It felt like heaven to me.

"Thank you for allowing me entry," I said.

She looked at me like I had spoken Chinese.

"I haven't seen anyone since the storm started. Figured everyone was snug at home or wherever they found some shelter." She looked me up and down. "You quite all right? You don't look too good."

"I just need a room for the night."

"That we got."

She went through a door on the other side of the chair and emerged a second later behind the check-in desk. She put a piece of paper down on the counter with a pen. "Just fill that in, please. We got a nice room for you. You'll like it."

I took up the pen, which felt foreign in my cold hand, like I was holding a piece of cooked pasta. I managed to write out my name on her form, and again I was struck—no, *invaded*—by the feeling that I was not where I thought myself to be. I was in some other universe. Perhaps in the afterlife and this woman was God, allowing me passage into heaven.

I looked up at her in the middle of writing down

my address. She gazed at me like I was now her favorite child. That made me feel warm inside, a feeling I fought to dispel. No point in developing a relationship with her. She was just the person who rented out rooms at a motel.

I made sure I put "Doctor" in front of my name. That usually got a reaction which benefited me. When I was finished, I put down the pen with perhaps more force than necessary. She took the paper and asked for my credit card. I fumbled in my pockets until I grasped my wallet and drew it out, flipped it open, and retrieved the plastic and handed it to her.

"Doctor, huh?"

"Yes," I said. "I have a practice in Portland."

"Don't much like doctors."

"Ah."

"Think they know everything. Every doctor I ever ran into thought his shit didn't stink and tried to tell me how to run my life when their own lives were sadder than a kid whose ice cream cone plopped on the ground."

"I see," I said.

"You think you know everything?"

"No Ma'am."

She beamed. "Glad to hear it. You usually travel with plastic bags for luggage?" She nodded toward my bag of foodstuffs. "Not that it's any of my business. Your car go off the road or something?"

"Something like that. I'm only glad you were here. You saved my life."

"Now don't get all dramatic. It's just a bed and a tv. Nothing grand or special. Just warm and dry." She put a key down on the counter. "Go outside and to your left."

I took up the key and thanked her and stepped into the outdoors one more time and my teeth resumed their dance and my skin started shivering again.

I found the room easily enough, red and beaten down, with a glaze of ice on the door. Ice encased the doorknob as well. I tried to knock it off with my hands, but it wouldn't budge and I couldn't get the key through the thickness of it. I used the key to chip away at the ice until I was able to insert the key into the lock. It turned, unlocking the door as best I could tell, but the knob wouldn't turn. Now completely frustrated and on my last thread of sanity, I stepped back, raised my foot, and brought it down on the door knob with all the force I could muster, which, by that time, was not very much at all. It had been too long a day and too long getting to the point where a warm bed was only a few feet from me.

On about the fourth kick, enough of the ice loosened so I could finally get inside. I expected a depressing room; that was the standard arrangement in such establishments, but what greeted me was beyond my imagination. The carpet was threadbare. The walls were dark wood paneling. The bedspread thin to the point of being translucent. I closed the door behind me and put my bag on the table in the corner. I dared not even think about what the bathroom might hold.

The table supported an old television, from the era when "flat screen" meant something one would see in a science fiction television program. I turned it on, if only to fill the room with something other than my own pathetic self. I found a Seattle television station and listened to reports of the ice storm as I sat on the edge of the bed and removed the strands of chain from my shoes.

What they were saying chilled me even more than the storm itself. No one in the weather business had ever seen a storm like this. No one in the weather business knew when it might clear up. The ice extended from northern British Columbia, all the way south to San Francisco, and went inland as far as Montana and

Wyoming. The entire west was shutting down as roads were necessarily closed to traffic and power outages were spreading rapidly as lines fell under the weight of the ice.

My feet were wet and cold. I took off my shoes and put my socks on the heater under the window, which was covered with ice, just like the door, so that all I saw through it was a collection of vague murky shapes, none of them in motion. The world had solidified into a collection of icy formations, completely foreign to me. I was hardly able to believe that I had been one of those shapes, sliding around the slick world, only a few minutes ago.

I phoned my office and left a message that I was going to be late tomorrow, not that it probably mattered. The city would likely be shut down and most people were not going to be able to make their appointments anyway. The emergency rooms, I hoped, would remain open. They were going to be doing brisk business. Probably already were, with car wreck injuries most likely piling people up like cordwood.

I pulled the sandwiches out of my bag and peeled off the plastic that wrapped them. The bread was not quite soaked all the way through, something I considered a minor triumph. The tomatoes were dried out and the lettuce was as limp as my wet socks. The turkey slices were more than a little suspect. Despite all this, I ate both sandwiches with gusto, savoring every bite as though it was my last.

Then I tossed a few pillows off the bed to the floor, took the one remaining, and leaned it against the head-board, which was sticky with *something* I didn't want to guess at. I leaned my head against the pillow and was asleep within a few minutes, but that did not last long. My dreams, which incorporated the faces of numerous women I have known, and numerous more I have want-ed to know, coalesced in a kaleidoscope of murky iced-over icons, splintered and cracked under the weight of an incessant kicking noise, which, as I climbed out of sleep like a truck straining to make a steep hill, soon dis-covered was coming from my own front door.

"Who is it?" I yelled to the air, completely uncaring about the volume of my voice. People could well have heard me two doors down, but I was still confused. Still unable to grasp exactly where I was.

"It's your favorite funny man." Tickles the Clown's voice. Muffled but unmistakable through the door.

I groaned. "What are you doing here?"

He kicked the door again. It rattled in its frame. The tv was still on. I fumbled around the bed, looking for the remote, found it, and muted the sound.

"Hey, you going to let me in or what?" More kicks. Louder and more insistent. Like he wanted me to be completely sure he was serious.

I debated my options. Leave the door closed and listen to him rant for a while until he went away or open the door and ruin the remainder of my night. I elected to try the former.

"I'm trying to sleep," I said. "Go away."

"I've got nowhere to go."

"Find another room."

"The lady said you got the last one."

Then he began a series of insistent and steady kicks to the door. I heard splintering and realized he was quite prepared to continue the procedure until he put his foot entirely through the door.

Finally, to save the door more than anything else, I pulled it open. He pushed his way past me, actually shoving me to the side, and stepped into the room. I saw that the weather was no better than before. In fact, the ice outside had only gotten thicker.

I closed the door and turned to face him, my mouth

set tight, and my arms folded across my chest.

"I was asleep," I said. "I need my rest. I need to be sharp for my patients."

He sat on the bed and picked up the tv remote. "Don't bullshit a bullshitter," he said. "You don't have any patients today or tomorrow. No one does. Haven't you been paying attention?"

"What happened to your party?"

"Got there and no one was home."

"So you came here."

"Where else was I going to go?"

"You could have gone back to the Humvee."

"You don't know what it's like out there now," he said. "It's much worse than it was. Besides, we destroyed the chains on that thing. It wasn't going anywhere."

I wanted to put him outside, I did, but he looked more miserable than I had felt earlier. My dormant sympathy instincts took over and I pulled a blanket out of the closet and tossed it on the waffle-like carpet. I kicked over a couple of pillows. "You're welcome to the floor," I said.

"Floor?"

"I paid for the room, I get the bed."

He tapped his forefinger against his thumb and

looked longingly at the bed. My bed.

"What?"

"That's a queen size bed."

"I'm not sharing a bed with you, so forget it."

"I'm not going to want to *do* you or anything, if that's what you're worried about."

"You stink," I said and instantly regretted it. My words hung in the air between us.

"You won't share a warm bed with someone lower class than you, is that it?"

I put my hand through my hair, not wanting to engage in this subject or this conversation.

"You could pretend I was one of your call girls."

I sighed. "You want the floor, or don't you?"

"I might get a morning erection, I grant you, since that still happens to me. Rarely, but still occasionally. But I wouldn't *do* anything with it. Not to you, anyway, so you don't have to worry. Truth is, you're kind of ugly. Did you ever notice? Like when you look in the mirror, haven't you seen how horribly unpleasant you look?"

Again, I felt rage begin to build in him, and I thought of how I might maneuver him out the door, but nothing came to me. He was clearly bigger than me, and more determined than me. And what was he asking, really?

What *was* I afraid of?

"You're right," I said. "There's plenty of room. If you take a quick shower, I'd be happy to share my bed with you."

His face instantly softened. "You mean it?" he said.

"Much as I wish I didn't."

He thumped me on the chest, as if to say "Thanks buddy!" and went into the bathroom, peeling off his shirt and pants as he went. I heard the plumbing squeak and presently the sound of spraying water filled the bathroom and leaked out into the room. I still heard the incessant tinkling sound of ice on the window, only it was not as sharp before. It had a quality of muffled softness to it now. It was as though a musician did not want to stop his set and continued playing the same tuneless melody over and over to infinity, but he was getting tired and he wasn't hitting the xylophone bars as hard as before. Didn't want the music to end.

I could barely see anything through the window any longer. The ice on the outside must have been inches thick by now. I worried about the roof over my head. About the roofs over everyone's head.

The sound of the shower stopped. Tickles the Clown emerged from the bathroom drying his hair with a towel. He had another towel hitched around his waist.

"Thanks for letting me in," he said, as pleasant as summer sun.

"No problem," I said. "Are you sleepy?"

"Actually," he said, "it *was* a problem, wasn't it?"

"I just had to adjust to having a roommate."

"We're more than roommates," he said. "Don't you realize what's happening?"

"We're in an ice storm."

He laughed. "Doctors," he said, and shook his head. "You don't know what's funny, that's your problem. See, me and you, hooking up together like this, two peas from different pods, it's damned funny. It's fucking *hilarious* that we should be buddies like this for the end of the world."

"End of the world?"

"It's what I've been saying, isn't it? Haven't you been listening?"

"It's just an ice storm."

"Once," said Tickles the Clown, "when I was, oh, I don't know, maybe nine years old. Maybe ten. My aunt told me a story. Aunt Maria. It's okay I'm telling you her real name because she's gone now. She told me that I would live to see the apocalypse. She told me she knew this because she had these visions. Ever since she was a little girl, she saw the future of things. Not *all* things. But some. She could tell if someone was going to live or die. Not *always*, understand, but enough of the time so that she knew it was an ability and not an accident. For example, she knew she was going to die in a couple of years, and she did. Got cancer a few months after she told me what I'm about to tell you, and lingered on for a while, but eventually died. Lung cancer, and she never smoked a single cigarette her whole life, so take that, mister doctor man, and shove it."

I remained as placid as I could manage, listening to him unspool his inept tale.

"Sorry," he said. "No offense meant."

"None taken," I said. By this time I had gotten into bed and had the covers pulled up around my neck. I felt absurdly like a child being told a bed time story, but the feeling was not foreign at all. It was as though we were meant to have this relationship, such as it was.

He rubbed his hair vigorously and tossed the towel to the floor. He stepped away from me and into the bathroom and returned wearing a pair of boxer shorts. I put out the light and felt the other side of the mattress depress as he got into bed.

He bounced around on the mattress, getting himself comfortable and situated while I endured his machinations in silence, which may have been a tactical error. I should probably have been more vocal about setting boundaries.

"Don't worry," he said after finally settling down completely. "I won't kiss you good night or anything. Way too tired. Ha!"

"I wasn't worried," I said.

"Where was I?"

"Your aunt Maria predicted the future."

"Oh, right. What she told me was I was going to witness the end and that I should not be alone when it happened. I was a little bit surprised, you can imagine."

"Sure."

"But I had no reason not to believe her. My mother told me her sister had always been like that, and she told Maria a long time ago that she didn't want her telling any of her predictions and she never did. To my mother. But to me she did. It was our secret, kind of, because I never told my parents. I knew they would be pissed."

"So your aunt talked about an ice storm?"

"Not exactly. She said the end was going to be cold. Not fire. Not hot death. Cold."

I tried to find some way into the conversation, so I could contribute and get him to see that he was delusional, but could not do so. Instead I asked him about his illness.

"Your cancer have anything to do with this doom and gloom attitude of yours?"

"Funny you should ask," he said. "When I got my cancer, I knew it was bad, but I also knew it wasn't going to kill me. Not right away, at least."

"How?"

"Simple. It was the middle of a heat wave. Hottest August ever."

"Yes," I said, "I remember that summer. People died from the heat."

"Yeah, poor fuckers stuck in their apartments, not knowing they were in danger. But it was hot, okay? That was the thing. I wasn't going to die because I hadn't witnessed the *cold* yet. Get it?"

"Sure," I said. "You did not yet fulfill your aunt's prophecy."

"Bingo," he said. "It gave me a lot of confidence, you know. Without my aunt's prediction, I might just have given up the fight and let myself die."

"That seems unlikely," I said.

"No, really. Cancer's a motherfucking bitch. You ever have it?"

I shook my head.

"Don't bother. It's worse than people say, even the people that went through it."

"I've seen patients afflicted with it."

"Not the same thing."

"I suppose not. Do you really think this is the end of the world?" I asked.

"Could be."

"You don't seem worried about it. You don't want to do something you've never done before? You don't want to contact people you love?"

He shrugged. The bed shook. I was going to feel his every move all night long. I did not look forward to the experience.

"And say what? Hey pal. Just wanted to say hi and bye since we're all going to be dead in a day or two."

"Well, sure, why not?"

The room was dark, and while the heater seemed to still be operating, there was a noticeable chill in the air, as though all the heat was looking for somewhere else to go. No part of my mind believed that any part of my world was coming to an end. And yet, something about this clown made me consider the possibility. At least for a moment.

"You know the funniest thing in the world?" said Tickles the Clown.

At first it seemed like an odd question. Upon quick reflection, I realized that it might be just the sort of thing a clown would think about as the end approached. If I truly believed the end was coming, what would I think about? My encounters with women who I paid to be intimate with me? No. That was ridiculous. Might just as well think about people who served me meals in restaurants. My parents? I had not seen them in three years. They were whiling away their golden years as desert rats in an RV town near Phoenix, Arizona, with other sun-dried oldsters, all of them tucked into their mobile homes like bats in their caves. Last time I went to see them, they wondered why I came. "Don't you have patients to get to?" my father said. "Don't want to keep you." He was so dark his smile seemed to glow from between his lips when he smiled at me.

"We don't have a lot of room in here, you know," said my mother. So I spent an afternoon, then returned to my patients.

"Dicks," said Tickles the Clown.

"What?"

"The funniest thing in the world. I've read about it. Anthropologists find that lots of women from all different cultures, especially the pre-industrial ones, when they get together, they laugh about our johnsons. It's universal. See, the way they dangle, the way they pop up unexpectedly, the shape of them. Absurd. Women know funny. That's why they laugh at our things."

"It's the end of the world and that's what you think about?"

"Is there a protocol for what we should think about in certain circumstances?"

"Don't you want to review your life? Take an assessment of where you've been? You're getting ready to sleep, and you're talking about dicks."

"I'm giving you the sum total of my wisdom. What better time than now? After tonight I won't be talking to anyone, me or you or anyone else. Also, why not sleep?"

"You can sleep when you're dead."

He laughed. The sound filled the room. It felt absurdly pleasant. Warm and comforting. Is that what people looked to clowns for? To funny people? Did they want that consolation? When sick kids came to me, my nurse often tried to make them laugh. I never saw the point. Laughter doesn't last. You feel better for a second or two, then it's over. I wanted medicine to make them feel better for good. But even my ministrations can only ever offer a temporary relief. Something gets you in the end.

"I can sleep when I'm dead?" said Tickles the Clown. "That's quite a saying. You make that one up?"

"Sorry," I said.

"You regret sitting next to me? On the bus? Do you wish you had picked that mother and her kid instead?"

"No regrets," I said.

"You should have some. Makes you human. You think you aren't human?"

"You're really a sad on the inside kind of clown, aren't you?"

He laughed again.

"I don't control my thoughts," he said. "They just come to me. It's like our dicks. Can't control the impulses they get, you know? That's why clowns have these big red noses. It reminds people of dicks, even if they don't realize it."

"That's absurd."

"Think what you think, but it's true. The more I behaved like a stupid man, the more laughs I got. The worst thing you can do is take yourself seriously."

"By that, you mean take my genitals seriously."

"Yup. Words of wisdom, my man. Take them to heart. All those working girls you spend time with. They laugh at you after they take your money and leave you alone. You ever think about that?"

"They have their lives, I have mine," I said.

"Sure, sure, I get it. A business transaction. No personal involvement. I understand all that, but I'm just saying. Is that you and them, they don't see the transaction the same way."

"I'm aware of that. It's the difference between customer and provider."

"No, no, that's where you're wrong. It's the difference between slave and master."

"Me being the slave."

"Bingo! You're brighter than you let on."

I let that remark hang in the air.

"In my clown days," he said, "I might have thought of an appropriate joke about now, spring it on you, and break the logjam I know has stopped up your brain about now, thinking about if I'm really as wise as I let on, or if I'm just being a dick myself, messing with your head."

"You're not 'messing with my head.'"

"Okay. If you say so. But someone is, I can hear it in your voice."

His voice was fading. He rolled over, away from me, to face the wood panel wall. I listened to the hum of the heater, trying valiantly to overcome the cold. I cheered on that heater, feeling a cold cavity in the pit of my stomach where warmth should have been pouring in. I closed my eyes, to try to encourage sleep, but the massive presence of Tickles the Clown beside me did not induce any sense of drowsiness. Tickles the Clown began snoring, a remarkable thing, to be able to sleep soundly on a night you think will be your last. I didn't know whether to admire his sangfroid, or hold contempt for his unwillingness to face the truth squarely. Or was he doing exactly that? Was it better to go about one's life, however mundane, no matter what, even in the face of doom?

I rose from the bed and went to the window and put my hand on the glass. It was cold. A thin layer of frost bit my palm. I welcomed the sensation, not knowing why. I had this vision of myself reaching into the storm and pulling something out of it. The truth? Maybe. Whatever that was. Or salvation? Weren't they the same thing? And why did I think I needed salvation?

I didn't. But maybe other people did.

I retrieved the phone book from the table by the bed and flipped through it to the yellow pages where I found the area hospitals. I called one, got an operator, and asked for the emergency room. A frantic sounding nurse answered.

"Are you open tonight?" I asked.

"Are we open? Of course we are."

"Do you have enough doctors?"

"Who is this?" Suspicion iced her words.

"I'm a doctor from out of town with nothing to do tonight. I'd like to help you out if you can use it."

"We can use every doctor we can get. Most of ours couldn't get in and patients are piling up."

"Can you send someone to pick me up?"

"Is this a joke, Doctor—?"

I told her my name. "No joke."

"I told you, our own staff can't get it. Patients are crawling to us if they have to. Our ambulances are stranded."

"Okay," I said. "I'll find my own way in."

She hung up without answering. I didn't blame her for thinking I was some kind of crank or crazy person.

That's what I would have thought. I looked at the map in the phone book to see how far away the hospital was. A little less than a mile, best I could determine. I didn't intend to walk that far. I was going to go to the Humvee and drive it over. It's true the clown and I raided its traction devices for our own ends, but it still had three tires chained up. That should be good enough for me to get to where I wanted to be.

I put my shoes back on and wrapped the strands of spiked chain around them. Tickles the Clown was sleeping quietly. I tiptoed around him as I retrieved my clothes and put them on. When I was as bundled up as I was going to be, I put my hand on the doorknob, turned it with some force and pushed on it. It wouldn't budge. I leaned back a little and applied my weight with a bit of acceleration behind it so my shoulder thumped it solidly and I heard ice crinkle and fall. I glanced over at Tickles the Clown. He was still as a cactus. Heavy sleeper.

I eased the door open and stepped into the cold ice, still falling. I surveyed the landscape. In another context, it would have been beautiful. Lovely layers of ice had transformed everything into an ethereal ghostly imitation of itself. It was as though the precipitation was a sculptor struck with wild bouts of inspiration that could not be contained. The buildings looked like iced cakes, the roads and sidewalks like translucent ribbons adorning a package, and the trees. Well. They reminded me of models of the circulatory system with their structural beauty until I shook off my training and instead saw them as gleaming stalks of light, bent into branch shapes and arranged like a bouquet by—who? I wanted to say God, but that was too absurd. I didn't believe in such a thing. Though I also knew it didn't matter. I was sure Tickles the Clown would say just because I didn't believe something, didn't mean it wasn't true.

I hear parents all the time, asking God for help to save their child. I do hear it. It sinks into me, this request. Like they think I am just an instrument of some mythical being. Sometimes it makes me feel good. Other times I wonder how they can be so ridiculous. If they think God can make their children better, then shouldn't they also believe God made their children sick?

The landscape seemed to be drinking up the ice, hungry for it, like a baby hungry for its mother's breast.

I tested my tractioned shoes, digging the spikes into the ice on the drive in front of the door. They held pretty good. I was able to stand without feeling like I was going to topple over, anyway. I started walking. I noted the light out in the office. The sky was dark. Streetlights were still on, so the power was holding in the city. That seemed a minor miracle in itself. There wasn't much of sidewalk here, just rough ground, now covered in undulating ice. I avoided its uneven and uninviting contours and went directly to the street, completely deserted except for me. I walked with a steady gait, my arms extended to hold my balance. Even though I was getting traction, I was also wary of falling. It would be no simple task to rise from the slick surface covering the world. It felt like a new skin was being applied to the Earth; a skin that repelled and invited at the same time. I imagined myself a tiny bug, rummaging around in the hide of the world, planting tiny stings with my barbed feet as I went. The Earth didn't seem to care, though. She gave no response to my miniscule machinations.

I got to the real estate office and went around to the back, where we had left the Humvee. It was still there, now gorgeous in its gleaming ice coat. It sported a good two or three inches of ice on all its surfaces. I have to admit, I hadn't thought much past finding the vehicle and driving it to the hospital. It had somehow slipped my mind that I would have to get the ice off the windshield if I was going to drive the vehicle.

I could have started up the engine and turned on the heater and let it melt the ice, but I knew from our earlier sojourn that that would take a long time, and I needed to get to the hospital if I was going to offer my help. My expertise. Such as it was.

It was not that I had no skills as a doctor, it was simply that I had chosen to let them atrophy. I had taken the easy road. Now I wanted to take the hard road. At least this one time.

I peered through the driver's door window but couldn't see far inside. The ice made everything into a shadowy silver-encrusted vista. Tickles the Clown had left the keys on the passenger seat. My plan, when I was under the covers back in the hotel room, was to break a window to get into the vehicle. But now I saw that was not going to be possible either. I had nothing to break the window with. Everything was frozen to the ground and covered in impenetrable ice. I saw a lump on the edge of the parking lot which was probably a good-sized rock, but it might just as well have been on the other side of the globe for all the good it could do me. I stood for a couple of long minutes while the ice built up on my head, shoulders, arms, and shoes. My feet were so numb from cold I could easily have believed I ended at my ankles. If I didn't move, I was going to be welded to my spot.

Reluctantly, I abandoned my idea of taking the Humvee, and instead turned back toward the dark street and began walking to town. It would take a little longer, but it wasn't that far, only a mile and traffic was extremely light so I was not hampered in any way by my fellow human being.

As I walked, the circulation in my leg began to improve. My feet were no longer numb. Instead they were tingling, as though waking from being asleep. Rising to the challenge, as it were.

One of the chains began to loosen and I began to slip on the ice. I had to attend to it, but I was afraid to stop and bend down. The ice was so slick that I might not be able to rise again.

I stopped. My breaths came in shallow bursts. My own heartbeat filled my head with noise. The ice continued to fall, a nightmare of coalescence going on around me. I looked around for an appropriate place to fix my traction devices and saw a gas station with a canopy covering its pumps. It was a mere quarter of a block distant. I hobbled to it, being very careful to not knock the chains completely off my unraveling foot. Not that my foot was unraveling. But it felt that way. It felt like my whole body was being torn apart by my journey through this ice. This infernal ice.

I felt myself falling into a fog of bewilderment and recognized it, vaguely, as a symptom of fatigue. Maybe depression as well. I gathered my strength as best I could and determined that I was going to finish my task. I stepped off the road and onto the sidewalk next to the gas station and encountered a strange lump there. It was perhaps a foot or so high, and extended in an oval shape, and had an uncanny suggestion of organic structure to it, as though whatever was under it possessed life. Or had once possessed life. Been alive.

I looked down at it, tried to peer through the ice, which, again, was futile. I couldn't see through this ice. I could only guess at what was behind it. It drank up all the meaning around it and transformed it into something else, into this blank nothingness.

Too small for a person, this lump must have been a cat. Or a small dog. Perhaps a raccoon? So hard to tell. Murky darkness tried to float out of the lump, but it was no more penetrable than a snow globe.

I looked up, as though the sky had some answers for

me. How could it? It was the sky.

I have seen babies die. I have pronounced babies dead. And yet. This dead cat or dog or whatever it was— I felt more for this creature, right then, than for any of my patients. This thought shamed me, but I pushed the shame away. I was good at that. I gingerly bent down, put my hand on the icy lump, closed my eyes for an instant, then rose as carefully and smoothly as possible and continued to the canopy at the gas station.

How much does ice weigh? A gallon of ice must weight less than a gallon of water, since water expands as it freezes, but still. Ice has a good weight to it. I got under the canopy and felt instant relief as I was no longer being pelted by icy precipitation. But at the same time I felt trepidation. All the ice that wasn't falling on me was falling on the canopy. I thought I heard creaks and groans from the supporting structure, but that could have been my imagination. I determined quickly that it might be to my advantage to keep my time under the canopy to a bare minimum.

I sat on the island, between two pumps, and worked to secure my lengths of spiked chain with the laces from my shoes. As I loosened them, I saw a smudge of red along one side where my blood had seeped into and stained my sock. I incorporated this information into my universe with remarkable calm, and only sought to investigate the cause of the bleed. I found it quickly enough: one of the spikes from the chain had worked itself through the leather of my shoe and punctured my foot. I must not have felt it earlier because my foot was cold and numb. I took my shoe off, removed my sock, and examined the wound. There was a hole there, no doubt about it. Looked like it went down a quarter inch or so. I looked up into the storefront of the gas station. There was almost certainly a first aid kit inside. Or should be. I hobbled over to the door and checked it, to see if it opened. It did not. I went back to the pumps, where I picked up a metal trash can which the establishment had left for its patrons, and raised it over my head and swung it down hard and fast onto the glass of the front door.

The trash can bounced off the glass and clattered against the pavement. I winced, thinking this was going to be a tougher job than I thought. I picked up the can and threw it at the glass with even more force, as much force as I could muster, and this time I cracked the glass. It displayed a jagged line like a lightning bolt. I kicked at the line with my other shoe and presently the glass began to give way even more, sprouting small cracks from top to bottom, tessellating the thing into a patchwork pattern. I kept kicking until my shoe went through the glass and I was able to reach in my hand and undo the latch that locked the door. I pulled the door open and stepped inside. Racks laden with candy bars, sodas, and bags of potato chips sat in the middle of the space like monoliths. I needed to attend to my wound, but in the meantime, I was ravenously hungry. I grabbed up some candy bars, ripped them out of their packages, and ate greedily and sloppily, like I was never going to eat again. After I had sated my hunger, I went behind the counter and bent down to look through the shelves. I found greasy gloves, some rags, piles of papers and receipts. I pulled some of them out and looked behind. Ah ha. Way in the back, behind a pair of pliers and some plastic spoons in little cellophane bags, a blue metal box. I yanked it out and saw a red cross on the lid. I stood up and put it on the counter.

"Find what you were looking for?"

The voice gave me chills. I looked up from the box and saw a man, a young man, no more than thirty, holding a shotgun aimed directly at my heart.

I instinctively put up my hands. "I'm not armed," I

said.

"I am," he said.

"I didn't know anyone was here."

"I didn't know anyone was crazy enough to be out on a night like this. I didn't want to try to get home in this storm, so I stayed here to look after the place. Seems I made the right decision."

"Look," I said, and coughed. My voice broke and fear pumped the biggest dose of adrenaline I have ever experienced through my body. My vision started to waver.

"I'm looking right at you," he said.

"I'm a doctor."

"Most doctors I know don't go around breaking into people's places of business."

"It's a strange night."

He lowered the shotgun so at least it wasn't aimed at me any longer. I felt instant, but not total relief.

"That it is," he said. "You got some ID? Keep in mind this firearm is loaded."

I slowly reached into my pocket and retrieved my wallet and pulled out my driver's license. I held it out for him to see. He walked closer, with the end of the shotgun wavering in the air like a frightened bee. He peered at the license. It showed my name, with the letters M and D after it.

He lowered his gun and looked at me. "Okay," he said. "I give up. What's a fancy pants doctor doing out on a night like this?"

"I was on my way to the hospital. They need doctors in the emergency room."

"Do tell?"

I nodded, feeling ridiculous.

"This isn't the hospital."

"I cut myself. I needed some first aid. I would have left money for the damage." I glanced over at the pile of glass near the door. Then I looked at him and noticed a door in the back that seemed to lead off to a small room. "Were you sleeping back there?"

"Yup."

"Sorry to wake you."

He studied me carefully. "You don't look sorry."

"I am."

"How you getting around in this? I don't see a truck out there, not that a truck would do you any good on a night like this. Or anyone any good."

I stepped out from behind the counter and showed him my shoe, the one with the chain pieces still attached.

He looked at it and pushed his lower lip out slightly and nodded. "I guess that would work. Like crampons. Them chains are illegal though. You know that?"

I nodded.

"Where'd you get them?"

"Took them off a Humvee."

"With the owner's permission, I assume."

I shook my head. I didn't see any point in fabricating a story. Might as well tell the truth and be out with it.

He laughed. "Vandalism and theft. You've had quite a night. Out of your comfort zone?"

I nodded.

"It's a long walk to the hospital," he said.

"I didn't have anything better to do tonight."

He put the shotgun down on the counter. "Let's see your wound," he said.

I showed him my other foot. He whistled. "Well, do what you have to do and get going."

"You going to call the police?"

"What for? They won't come out tonight. They can't."

I opened the first aid kit and pulled out a tube of antiseptic cream and a bandage.

"Those chains secure on your feet?" he asked.

"They could be better," I said.

"Let me see what I can find."

"Thanks," I said.

"Don't mention it," he said. "I feel like we're family, don't you?"

I looked up at him, and dredged up a quote from somewhere long ago, something about all humans being part of the same family, so being kind was important. I didn't remember the exact wording, though, and mangled it in the telling.

"You are one peculiar doctor, I'll say that," he said and disappeared through the door into the garage.

I couldn't disagree.

I went into the tiny bathroom at the back of the store and put my foot up into the sink and ran hot water over it with some pink soap granules from the dispenser on the wall. My wound stung, but it wasn't terrible. I could walk on it. I applied the cream to it and covered it with one of the larger bandages from the first aid kit. When I emerged from the bathroom into the store again, the owner had a pair of boots in his hands and some lengths of plastic fasteners.

"These look like they'd fit you," he said. "You can't be out there in those." He nodded at my shoes. I had to admit, they were inadequate to the task.

I sat down on the chair he had behind the checkout counter and put the boots on. They were a little snug, but would do for the journey I had in mind. He bent down and helped me wrap the chain segments around them. I had a peculiar sensation of tenderness toward him and anyone who helps a stranger, who takes a chance on someone he doesn't know. For all he knew, he was risking his life by having me in his establishment, but he was still willing to aid me in my endeavors.

"These boots are made of thicker leather than your shoes," he said. "Should keep the hooks from digging into you."

"Thanks," I said.

He didn't answer, just secured the chains with the plastic fasteners. One end of each looped through a hole in the other end and didn't loop back. It contained a sharp bit of metal that prevented the loop from loosening. He tugged on the ends so they wrapped good and tight.

"That should do you better than what you had before," he said. "Sorry I don't have crampons in the shop." He looked up and grinned. "Not much call for mountain climbing equipment around here."

"I can imagine. What do I owe you?"

His face didn't exactly darken, but some of the good feeling we had generated leaked out of the proceedings.

"As I understand it," he said, "you're on a mission of mercy. Did I get that right?"

"Yes."

He stood up and looked me over, like I was a wet dog. I felt like a wet dog. "Then there's no monetary issue involved. Next time, though, think about knocking, hmmm?"

Before I could answer, a report like a gunshot rang through the store. We both froze as another colossal crack, from somewhere outside, seemed to kick us both in the gut. He saw the motion first, the canopy outside sway ever so slightly, a delicate movement, like a ballet dancer adjusting her feet with a minute nudge. My benefactor grabbed me by the arm and pulled me through the store to the back, where I saw a cot flash by and another door beyond it, which he pushed open into the storm once again, the ice still falling. He held onto me as his feet slid and wobbled under him and I, outfitted in my traction devices, held firm and tall, solid, until a colossal sound of crumpling metal and snapping concrete filled the air.

We looked at each other, then silently walked around the building to the front, where we saw the canopy had crashed away from the store.

"Luck's with me tonight," he said.

"If you call that luck," I said.

"I'm still alive. So are you. I call that lucky. Now get going. I want to get more sleep tonight."

I escorted him back to the front door and he stepped onto the broken glass, tinkling the air with crystal pops and snaps, and then allowed the door to close between us. I didn't want to leave him.

"You going to be okay?" I said.

"I got a heater back there."

"There's a guy."

He raised his eyebrows. "Yeah?"

"We sort of got thrown together and he kind of latched onto me. He might come looking for me. If he does, don't tell him where I am."

"Secret mission, huh?" He grinned again. I realized that I was going to miss his grin, which fact seemed more than a little absurd.

"Hang on a sec," he said, and went to the shelves and grabbed a few candy bars and handed them to me. "For energy," he said. "Not that they're particularly healthy, but you need something."

I thanked him, turned, stepped around the canopy, which, now that it was down, imparted to my being a sense of safety, seeing as how it could not fall again, and reconnected with my trail.

The streetlights began flickering. They were fighting against the black anyway, but they gave some illumination to light my path. Not to mention a feeling of security. As long as the electricity held out, I had the feeling I could believe this storm was only temporary. If power went away, then maybe that was the first step towards the end, and maybe Tickles the Clown knew what he was talking about after all.

I did see some lines down as I passed some smaller streets that crossed my road. Trees had also crumpled and fallen. I noticed some roofs had collapsed, the flat variety, which, obviously, had never been designed to hold up tons of ice. Tons? Had to be. There was so much of it. I looked down at my feet, stepping over ice that looked to be at least three inches thick. Maybe four or five. And more accumulating all the time.

I looked up, returning my gaze to the path in front of me, and just as I did so, the streetlights flickered once more, then gave out completely. An ominous darkness descended on everything at once. There was a moon out this night. I saw its mark, a blurry patch of white, barely visible through the black, but it was now the only illumination I had. Except, I soon saw, for the ice. The ice reflected up some light into the air. Not a lot, but enough to tell me the Earth was still there, somewhere outside of me, laid out like a cold blanket. It was almost as if the ice contained phosphorescent particles. Was it possible?

The hooks under my feet bit into the ice. The squeals and scrapes and squeaks of metal impaling and lacerating ice sent shivers up my spine, which, considering how cold I felt, was no small thing in itself.

Up ahead, somewhat out of my clear vision, I saw a shape. It loomed dark and big. A creature, of some kind, certainly. Bigger than a person. I stopped, unsure what to do. What else would be out tonight? Whatever was there in front of me stopped as well, probably about a block away. My chest heaved up and down. My throat felt raw and my lungs hurt. The barbs under my feet squeaked on the ice as I shifted my weight slightly. We stood for what seemed like five minutes or more, long enough for both of us to grow weary of the standoff, I suppose, because eventually we both began moving forward. I with tentative steps, the—*something*—with slow plodding steps of its own. Presently I discerned the shape of the thing more fully: it was big and round, muscular. It had a fairly long snout. And paws. Big wide paws that spread out in front of it. Part of me knew exactly what it was long before the rest of me caught up and accepted the simple fact that what I was seeing, advancing toward me, was nothing more or less than a bear. It used its claws to dig into the ice and make progress, much as I was doing with my makeshift crampons. It had a comical air about it, this big animal proceeding gingerly across the crystal scape that the world had become. Was becoming.

It saw me, but did not want to engage me, or so I hoped. I further hoped that I was presenting an unappetizing prospect, because if it took a mind to attack and eat me, there was nothing I could do to prevent it. I was vaguely aware of some advice I once read about what one should do when confronting a bear. If it was a brown bear, it was best to climb a tree. Obviously that was advice for people in the woods. No trees at hand in apocalyptic Olympia. I suppose, if the situation called for it, I could try to make a run to one of the houses or buildings nearby and break in. Barricade myself on the other side of a door. Except I was sure the bear could outrun me.

Further advice, dredged up from my memory: If the bear was a black bear, don't bother climbing a tree because they can climb trees too, and will. In that case, your best chance, if attacked, is to lie on the ground, curled up in a fetal position, with your hands over your head to protect your face and skull. Even when I read this it seemed like particularly poor survival advice. If the bear was serious, then, sure, *maybe* you might survive, but you also might not *want* to at that point.

And what about the bear? What kind of advice did the ursine community offer to each other upon meeting humans? The bear got close enough for me to see its eyes. They glowed, ever so slightly, in the night, reflecting the strange illumination coming up from the ice.

I saw—or *thought* I saw—that it had no interest in me. I was a piece of vegetation it was passing by.

I had never been so close to such a powerful animal. It advanced upon my position slowly, deliberately. The ice shook with each step, and its panting breath filled the air and my ears. My entire body shivered. I felt the hairs on my arms and my back rise and—so it seemed to me—tingle with the feeling of this creature's power snaking into my being. My heart rate increased tremendously. I stopped and watched. There was little else I could do. I saw iridescent filaments of ice clinging to its fur. It stopped, once, to shake itself, as though growing weary of the extra weight of the ice, and the sound of it, like a million stones on a necklace clinking one against the other, filled my world. I was ready to bow down to this creature. I was ready to do its bidding.

"What are you telling me?" I whispered to it.

It didn't acknowledge me or my question. Instead it kept walking. It would have walked right over me if I had not taken two steps to the side. I did so, and it passed within a foot of me. Without thinking, I put out my hand and pressed my palm, for an instant, onto its fur. I felt moisture, ice shards, and heat. A rippling muscle, solid as rock. Contact of a kind I had never known. An intimacy that circulated comprehension through my being like blood through a network of vessels.

This bear *knew* something I did not. Maybe it knew what was happening. Maybe it was going somewhere I should be going.

It stopped and snorted at the air. Then it squatted and strained for a second or two and deposited a substantial load onto the ice that steamed thick billows into the air, as though this pile of shit had to release its energy or it would explode.

Then the bear leaned forward again and resumed its walk, entirely oblivious to me and my meandering mind attempting to come to terms with the meaning of my encounter.

Ha! as Tickles the Clown might say. What meaning? There was no meaning. Only two animals passing in the night.

I looked back at the bear's rump receding into the darkness, wobbling from side to side.

Okay, bear, I thought. You have your place to get to. I have mine.

I had some difficulty removing my boots from the ice. Even for the short time that I was standing there, waiting for the bear to pass, the falling ice had begun to weld me to the ice already on the ground. I pulled at my boots, felt my feet slipping out of them slightly, and stopped pulling. No sense in standing there in sock feet. I bent my leg to one side, then the other, trying to extract the boots from the hold the ice had on them. A cold realization dawned on me, that I was not going to be able to do this on my own, and for at least the third time that night, maybe the fourth or fifth, panic gripped me. Was I going to die here, a cold sculpture of myself executed in ice?

I yanked again. No good.

I bent down and struck the side of my boot with my fist. I felt the hits in my feet, but they did nothing to dislodge the boot. I hung there, with my chest down over my thighs, and my head folded down by my knees, as though I was executing some absurd yoga pose, and decided I was prepared to die.

This stance was new to me. I had never before made the decision to accept my death, even though my profession brought me within proximity to death on a regular basis. But what I didn't tell Tickles the Clown, when I was recounting my sad life story, was that my mediocre performance in my job was due to my fear of death. What he didn't understand was that my constant need for attention from prostitutes was my way of overcoming that fear.

More to the point, I did not realize it until that moment, inhaling the fumes of a bear's droppings while ice welded me to the ground. Could there be a less dignified ending to one's life? At that moment, it was difficult to imagine, though now, writing this account months later, I would have preferred that ending to any number

I could imagine in its place.

An image of my mother came to me, completely unbidden, and this struck fear into my heart. If I was seeing her, at this time, in this place, under these circumstances, surely it meant the end was near. My life flashing before me. I saw my mother as she looked in a picture I had of her soon after I was born. Radiant with the glow of having birthed me. Or so I flattered myself. At that moment, with ice encrusting my body, I wanted only her warm touch. I needed her to wrap me in her softness. I began to weep at the thought that I had never felt that comfort since I was a young boy. And comfort is what I sought, always. Comfort is our eternal quest as a species and as individuals.

I tried to remember what the timeline was for death by exposure. I could not dredge it out of my frozen memory. I wanted to lie down. I thought of the last few days, the time I spent in my own private brand of debauchery.

Did I regret it? A little. But not a great deal. I reflected that such thoughts were somewhat ridiculous, given my imminent demise. Should I instead give some thought to what happens after death? Didn't my wretched and neglected soul need some attention?

I was thus engaged in such unproductive musings when I heard a loud snort behind me. Then hair-raising snuffling and the sharp sound of claws on ice.

The bear had developed second thoughts.

I lifted myself from my folded position and was just about to rotate my hips to allow myself to see this bear and what it might be up to, when I felt a sharp slap at my ankles.

I call it a slap, but it was more than that. It was a swipe. It tore through the ice at my shoes and knocked me completely over. I heard something snap. I hoped it was the ice, and not one or more of my bones. I found myself face down on the ice and completely forgot the tip about curling up and protecting my skull. Instead, I turned over to face my executioner. It stood on all fours and stared at me. I could not look away from it. Did not *want* to look away from it, or its eyes, or it's drooling mouth. It bared its teeth at me, and panted heat into the air. My brain, wild with fear, groped through the mind field of creation, in an attempt to find something—*any-thing*—to use in my defense.

"I'm a doctor, don't kill me."

"I'm old. I'm tough. Don't eat me."

"I'm a spiritual being. Don't snuff out my divine essence."

"I'm scared, I'm scared, I'm scared."

But on the evidence, I had to conclude that the bear had no interest in me beyond tossing me to the ground. After regarding me for some few moments, it took a step back, rose up on its hind legs, roared into the air, then went back to all fours and turned and ambled off again.

Well.

I didn't know if I should thank the beast or be mad.

I elected to express my anger. I groped for its pile, grabbed up a good chunk of it, rose up on my feet, and threw it at the bear. I missed. It landed with a plop a good ten feet behind the beast. I was not much given to acts of desperation, but the situation seemed to call for it. I grabbed up another good sized portion of its mess, (remarkably cohesive, I noted in passing) and threw again, with as much might as I could muster. This missile disintegrated in the air as it arced high, becoming several smaller nuggets, most of which fell to one side of the bear, but a few connected, hit its icy fur, and slid off to the ground. The bear didn't notice a thing, just kept lumbering away.

Stupid bear.

That saved my life.

I felt something liquid on my upper lip and brought my hand—my *other* hand, not the one engaged in missile warfare—to my face and realized blood was coming from my nose. It must have happened when I got knocked down. I dragged my sleeve over my nose and upper lip. Then I brought my attention to my feet. The bear had dislodged me alright, but it had not done so without a certain amount of damage. The traction devices on my left boot had torn through the edges of the leather and separated the forward section of the sole from the upper portion of the boot. In fact, as I took a few practice steps, I saw that the sole flopped wildly. That was going to present a few challenges for walking. The dumb thing had also contrived to tear the lower portion of my pants with its claws, so that it hung in tattered shreds.

No matter, I told myself. I would press on. The bandages I had applied to my previous injury still held, as far as I could tell. I was not going to remove my boot to look at it now. There would be time for that later.

I took a deep breath, adjusted my shoulders, and kept walking, my boot sole flapping in the air, and my head swimming with possibilities. I had been given a reprieve. A gift from a bear. A tough love swipe.

And I needed to be worthy of that.

Didn't I?

Maybe not. A few minutes later, the incident safely locked away in my memory vaults, I was able to return to my old cynical self. Thank goodness for the slippery goodness of memories. Nothing more comforting in the world than the knowledge that trauma slides away on its own.

I encountered no other living being for the next half hour or so. For this I was grateful. I heard many things: snapping limbs, falling power lines, roofs collapsing, and that incessant white noise of the falling ice, an infernal humming and static, blurring all else with its obliterating crackles.

Pain had overtaken much of my lower extremities. I had cuts and bruises, which contributed, but even without those, my constant hobbling gave me twinges of constant pain. I knew I needed treatment, but in the grand scheme of the end of the world, they were minor ailments.

I had lost my sense of time, but the sky was not lightening up at all, so I assumed it was not yet near dawn. But I couldn't be sure. I did see a very faint glow ahead of me, over the horizon, which I assumed had to be the hospital. The power was out in town, but the hospital, which would have its own generator, maintained a light for the world. I hurried as best I could toward that light, through neighborhoods, over iced streets, and across lumpy sidewalks.

A deer crossed my path. It sprang out of a backyard and skittered through the air and over the ice in front of me. I laughed at its antics. My nose ran. I tried to clean it with my sleeve, but all I managed to do was smear the blood and snot over my face. I found I didn't care, which gave me pause. It only took a few hours of disruption in my life to turn me into a savage? A low-grade savage, granted, but even so, the thought did give me pause to consider.

Perhaps the world didn't have to end completely for people to take leave of their civilized senses and retreat to some barbaric comfort zone where life was basic: step, step, step. Pause. Eat. Step step step step.

Oh.

Eat. Yes. I was hungry. I reached into my pocket and retrieved two of the candy bars the kind man at the gas station had given me. I tore open the wrappers and discarded them. Was I littering? Yes. Did I care? A little. But not enough to pick up the wrappers. I ate the candy bars ravenously, with gusto, the muck of the chocolate wrapping itself around my tongue and teeth. Sugar shot through my system. Or, at least, it felt like sugar shot through my system. I knew better. The sugar had to go through my digestive system. But the charge from the candy bars was not disputable. I felt better. Immensely better. I could take on the world if I had to. I could practice my profession again.

I imagined what cases and patients I might have to attend to when I got to the emergency room. I had never done emergency medicine, but I knew colleagues who did. It was a lot of intuition, as I understood it. You made quick decisions about diagnosis and went with your gut. I was good at that. I was in a life or death business. I knew that. It was why people trusted me. Often, when they came to me, they had exhausted all other option in their lives. Their children—their *children!*—needed care and they had heard from someone that I was at least competent. Or they had simply looked me up in the phone book. Or or or. Who knew how people chose doctors? A dart and a dart board, for all I knew. But something happened to me the first time a patient of mine died. It wasn't my fault. Not by a long shot. The poor boy had cancer and there was nothing anyone could do. I referred him to an oncologist but he did not last more than a few months.

The parents *thanked* me. I didn't know how to respond. I didn't know why they thanked me, for one thing. They brought their son to me, and soon after that he was dead.

The thank you was especially devastating, because when I heard he died, I gave up.

Not completely. And not right away. Certainly not that anyone could tell, but whatever passion I had for medicine evaporated.

I went through the motions. I pretended to care. *Pretended.* Other doctors I know turned to drugs or drink in similar circumstances. We were the fallen idealists. The ones who couldn't stand the simple fact that we could not save everyone. I had never been much interested in mind-altering substance, and instead turned to women to assuage my feelings of inadequacy and my inability to accept death. In their embraces, strangely warm and cold at the same time, I found some brief comfort and my time with them became an addiction and an obsession.

The ones I met and engaged for my shameful needs were also some of the smartest people I knew. I fooled a lot of people into believing I was a good doctor: my patients, their parents, my nurses, my colleagues, and so on. But not the call girls. They saw right through me. One of them begged me to reconsider my profession. She said if I didn't have passion for my work, I should find other work.

Such wisdom! Especially considering the source. I asked her if she had passion for her work. She told me yes, of course, why else would anyone do what she did.

"For the money, of course," I told her.

"Money only takes you so far," she said. "You can't let money rule your life."

Ah, but I did let it rule my life. I craved the creature comforts and didn't want to lose them. I needed money to engage the wise women who satisfied my urges without delving too deeply into my heart. Insulating myself from the world took means. And I had the perfect opportunity to attain those means.

I tell you all this, at this point in the narrative, to offer some picture of my mental state at the time I approached the light from the hospital. It was as though the medical building was a beacon of faith, calling me forward and pulling me out of my self-imposed, and selfish, mental state.

Now imagine my surprise and consternation as I got even closer to the light and through the murky darkness of that abominable night I saw not what I expected, which was a gleaming modern edifice of a medical center, complete with brick façade, glass accents, and impeccable landscaping, and instead saw that I had been led to a neighborhood clinic. A small box of a building on the corner. The type of place that triaged minor injuries and sent the worst cases on to the *real* hospital, which, obviously, I had no idea where it might me.

I stopped and stood, staring, at this tired-looking wooden dump. I say dump, because that is what it looked like to me. The parking lot, I could see, even covered by thick ice, had cracks and upheavals in it, completely in need of repair. The exterior walls were of wood, and somewhat dilapidated wood at that, with peeling paint and a distinct drabness to the whole enterprise that gave it a thoroughly uninspiring air, as though only zombies would give themselves to such an institution. A neon OPEN sign flickered in the window.

I wanted to go elsewhere, but where else would I go?

I dragged my flopping boot across the ice, hobbling all the way. At the entrance I pushed the door open and stepped inside. I fully expected to see patients, at least a few, and a receptionist. Instead, I was presented with an empty waiting room, and no one behind the admission desk, which, itself, was nothing more than a wooden desk piled high with papers and supporting an enormously bulky computer terminal of the type I thought had gone out of favor at least a decade ago.

A woman I took to be a doctor came out of a back area. She wore the white coat many of us seem to favor, and she greeted me with an outstretched hand.

"Hello," she said. "How are you. We don't get many clowns here at the clinic."

Clown? "I'm not a clown," I said.

She held up her hands. "Sorry," she said. "Didn't mean to offend. It's just the big red nose—" she pointed at my face "—and the floppy shoes—" she pointed at my boots "—and the baggy pants." She shrugged. "I just thought."

I felt not anger, but a deep weariness, rise up from some remote recess in my belly. My pants were *not* baggy. Torn up a bit, yes. Perhaps with a comical accent to them. But certainly not *clown* pants.

I sighed. I had gone so far. Now that I was here, I couldn't remember why it was so important to *be* here.

"So," she said. "My name is Doctor Zane. The sanest doctor you'll ever meet." She grinned. "We're short-handed because of the storm, but I'm here to help. What seems to be the problem?"

"No," I said. "I'm not a patient. I'm a doctor. I understood, or, that is, I was told that you needed medical professionals here."

She spoke gently, probably as gently as she ever had to anyone. "I see. Well, I'm glad you're here to help. But I see you do have some injuries. May I attend to them, please? That way you will be in tip top shape to help me when the real patients begin arriving. They don't usually come in *during* a storm. It's when it stops that we get slammed. Falls, car wrecks, stress induced heart attacks. That sort of thing."

I nodded. "I know," I said. "I know that's what happens during and after storms. I *know*."

She nodded at me and smiled.

I fumbled in my pocket for the ID that would *prove* I had medical training. The driver's license with the MD after my name. My two letters of significance. My identification with the elevated class of humanity. I was a professional of some stature and I needed to convey this fact to Dr. Zane. But I could not find that rectangle of plastic. I checked all my pockets. I dripped blood as

I bent my head down. I found I didn't care. Blood and snot could drip out of my nose forever. It didn't matter. Not anymore.

I looked up at her. She did have a kind face. She did present some aspect of benevolence that I may have needed at that time. I dropped my hands, as though saying: "I give up the search. I am in your hands."

And so I became a patient for the first time in my life. We entered a tiny examination room. Doctor Zane took my medical history, which was not particularly extensive as I have had few ill days during my existence, and no major medical issues of any kind.

"You trying to live to a hundred?" she asked. "Because at the rate you're going, you should make it easily." She beamed.

"Thanks," I said.

"Now let's get you out of those clothes and take a look at your injuries. How did you get those nasty gouges in your leg?"

"A bear," I said.

"From your act?"

I looked at her. She had a sparkle in her eyes. Was she mocking me? Or was she one of those eternally cheerful people?

"Yes," I said. "From my act."

"I'm thinking maybe you should fire that bear, huh? I wouldn't want a bear like that in my act. Too dangerous. What do you think?"

"Yes," I said. "Perhaps I should fire that bear."

She grinned. I heard the front door open and close.

"Oops," she said. "Another customer, it looks like. I'll be right back."

She left the little examination room and I took off my shoes and socks, now red from blood, and removed the dressing on my foot. The wound was not infected, as far as I could tell, but it did look nasty. I took off my pants and shirt and put on the red smock Doctor Zane had left for me on the counter.

A mirror hung on the door. I looked at myself. I had to admit, I did present a certain clownish aspect. My hair was disheveled, my nose still presented a distinctly reddish hue, and my costume would be considered comical by any common standard.

The door swung open. I stepped back. Doctor Zane stood in the doorway, holding my driver's license in front of her. She looked from the license to me and back to my license again. "Well, I'll be," she said. "You really are a doctor."

"Yes, I am," I said. "Where did you get that?"

Before she could answer two police officers came up behind her and barged their way into the examination room. They wore crampons on their feet, actual metal ice-walking devices, which I envied immediately. I would have loved to have had such things for my journey across the ice. I noted their name tags: officers Simons and Robertson. Robertson spoke first. "Good morning Doctor. We'd like to ask you a few questions."

By this time Zane had retreated into the hall but I still saw her face, simultaneously awed, annoyed, and bemused, peeking from between the shoulders of the cops.

"Do you know a Conrad Hartley?" asked officer Simons while Robertson bent down and picked up the lengths of chain that had gotten me to the clinic over the sheets of ice covering Olympia.

"No," I said. "What's this about?"

"Mr. Hartley was found dead in a motel room rented by you."

Robertson stood up. Both cops stared at me.

"You mean Tickles," I said.

"Tickles?"

"That's his stage name. He's a clown. Tickles the

124

Clown."

Simons scratched his chin.

Robertson studied me like I was a disease he needed to identify. "That a fact?" he said.

"Yes," I said. "Tickles is dead? Really?"

"Got a report from the owner of the motel. It also appears you've been on some kind of crime spree. You and—Tickles—stealing a car, vandalizing said car, and breaking into a place of business. You care to explain all that?"

"I was trying to get to work," I said. "I needed to practice medicine." I felt the absurdity of the statement immediately, but could not retract it, much to my regret.

"You work here?" said Simons.

"In Portland," I said. "But the storm stuck me here."

"You're quite a way from Portland," said Robertson.

I liked their tag team questioning. It had a certain balletic quality to it, like they had rehearsed the moves and knew each other's style.

"I use my skills where they're needed."

Simons raised his eyebrow. "Doctor Zane here doesn't believe you're a doctor. Thinks you're some kind of entertainer."

"A clown," said Zane, speaking up from behind the

officers. "I *thought* he was a clown, but I don't think so anymore."

Robertson and Simons heard her, but chose to pretend they did not.

"I'm sorry to hear Tickles died," I said.

"The man left a note. We think it was meant for you."

I nodded. They didn't offer me the note they referred to. They kept looking at me, studying me and my reactions. I thought they must have had better things to do than waste their time with me. Weren't there accidents to attend to? Murders committed by people driven crazy by the monotonous sound of falling ice? Weren't there people all over town that required attention much more than I did?

"Am I allowed to see the note?" I said.

"Do you know," said Simons, "that you look kind of like a clown?"

I inhaled a long breath, held it, then released it. "I'm pretty sure," I said, "that in a former lifetime, I was a clown. In fact, I'm pretty sure we all were, and we like to wear uniforms because it reminds us of what we once were, what we once aspired to."

My attempt at making them see themselves differently, for even a moment, was lost on them both, although I think I saw Zane nodding behind them with the light of recognition in her eyes. She took the lapels of her white coat in her hands and brought them together tightly around her chest.

Simons finally pulled a wad of paper from his pocket and handed it over to me. It contained several sheets with the name of the motel printed at the top in pale blue letters. I put them down on the counter and smoothed them out with my hands and began reading.

"Dear Doc:

"I woke up and you were gone. Was it something I said? Ha!

"I'll write here until I can't anymore. I took a bottle of pills and they'll be acting pretty quick, so I'll be writing pretty quick to get my last thoughts down.

"I wanted my final night in this realm to be with at least one other member of humanity, but maybe that was too much to ask. We all die alone, don't we? No one shares that experience with us.

"Anyway, I just wanted to tell you how much the last few hours meant to me. I wish I had had children, so I could have passed on my wisdom to them. Never happened. So I made other people's children laugh instead. You too, I think. Not the laughing part, but you had no children of your own, so you took care of other people's. Filled a void. Am I right? I think so. No accident, Doc, that we ended up together on this night, shooting the breeze, comparing professional notes, coming to terms with death and so on.

"But now my journey's ended. The cancer came back, you know. I didn't tell you that, but I'm sure, a medical man like yourself, you knew. On some level. The same way I know if something's funny or not: by instinct. I don't *feel* the funny anymore, like I told you, but I *know* the funny. Always know exactly what makes people laugh.

"Only this cancer took some of that away and I can't fight it anymore. Better to bow out now, before I get really feeble and pathetic and droolly.

"I'm sure that goes against your doctor instincts. You want to keep people alive no matter what. Don't you? Well, I hope so, otherwise you'd be a damn piss poor doctor, right? But maybe, on some level you wanted me dead. Knew I'd kill myself if you left the room. Remember, I asked you, did you ever want to kill one of your patients? What do you think? Maybe I was right, huh?

"But, anyway. What does it matter? Sometimes we don't need doctors. We just need warm bodies next to us, holding our hands, telling us everything is going to be okay. Even if it isn't. Sometimes *especially* if it isn't.

"Wish I had a bottle of whiskey about now. Didn't think that one through. Should have bought one in Seattle before we left.

"Not much time left. Darkness everywhere. The damned ice. Choking everything. Maybe it'll keep me out of hell, you know. Maybe this is hell freezing over. You think?

"Probably not.

"Remember what we talked about. That thing we mentioned. How it's funny? You got to have a sense of humor about yourself. You got to, or you're dead. Take it from me. I know.

"So. You're still young Doc. You still got time to become a real human being. Someone who doesn't hire other people for companionship, you know. Someone who makes real connections.

"Like you did with me.

"Even if you think you didn't."

He signed it: "Chuckles and Laughs from Tickles the Clown." Underneath, in a crooked line, he had drawn the face of a clown with an enormous nose.

I finished the pages and looked up at the officers.

"He's really dead?" I asked.

They never took their eyes off me. "That's right," said Simons. They stared at me some more.

Then I saw what they were doing. They wanted to know if I had a hand in Tickles's death. "He was just a guy I met on the bus," I said. "I didn't know him. Certainly didn't want him dead."

"You guys shared a room," said Simons.

"It was the storm," I said. "The storm brought us together. Completely by chance."

"The storm?" said Robinson

I nodded. "He thought it was the end of the world." I paused. "I guess he was right. At least for him."

Officers Simons and Robinson were silent for a few more seconds, then took the pages back.

"We'll keep this for evidence," said Simons.

"Good idea," I said.

"Next time you need to get to work, find a better way," said Robertson.

"I will, officer," I said.

"Also, don't think this is over. You're going to have to answer for that stolen vehicle. After this crisis is over, and you've finished with your docotoring, we'll come back for you. Don't leave town, got it?"

I nodded. "I won't, officer," I said.

They turned and went out of the examination room and into the hall. Zane stepped aside to let them by.

I felt, inexplicably, like I had never been more alone in my life.

Doctor Zane came into the room. "Well," she said. "Not often we get a visit from the local constabulary. Everything okay?"

I nodded and put out my hand, hoping she would take it.

About the Author

Mario Milosevic has published poems, short stories, and novels in numerous venues, both print and online. He lives in the Pacific Northwest, but so far has not experienced an ice storm of the proportions described in *The Doctor and The Clown*. Learn more about the author and his work at mariowrites.com.